DARK SKIES: A KERRIGAN SURVIVAL SAGA

ECHOES

—— OF THE ——

FALLEN

MATT GROOVER'S TALE

JOSEPH SACKETT

To My Friend Matt

To Matt Groover,

In the tapestry of life, we often cross paths with individuals who leave indelible marks on our souls. You, Matt, are one such person. Your journey, a testament of courage and resilience, has been the guiding star in the creation of this narrative.

Serving in the 101st Airborne, you faced the tempests of the Iraq War with a bravery that goes beyond words. The tales of your experiences, woven with threads of valor and fortitude, have been the inspiration behind the character that now breathes life in the pages of this series.

Your story, marked by the trials of war and the unyielding spirit of a soldier, has been a beacon of inspiration. In crafting this character, I have sought not just to tell a story, but to honor the essence of a friend whose life epitomizes the strength of the human spirit.

Matt, your friendship has been a light in the darkest of times. You are more than a comrade-in-arms; you are a friend for life. Your unwavering support and genuine kindness have been the pillars upon which this journey was built.

With this book, "Echoes of the Fallen," I pay homage to you. Thank you for being you—your courage, your strength, and your heart. You have not only inspired a character but have left an indelible mark on my life.

May this story serve as a reflection of our friendship and a tribute to your extraordinary journey.

With deepest gratitude and respect,

Joseph Sackett

Contents

Prologue

In Iraq's vast desert, Matt Groover stood alone, eyes sweeping over an endless landscape of sand and rock. The hot wind was his only companion in the profound silence. Far from his old world, this barren land had become his reality since joining the 101st Airborne Division.

Looking across the desert, he felt an eerie stillness, hinting at hidden, unspoken truths. It was a moment of calm before the unknown, the desert's timeless face reflecting an imminent change. His story, etched in the harsh reality of a soldier's life, began here. A story where death's shadow was ever-present, an unwelcome guest at every turn.

In this desert heartland, tranquility was deceptive. Each grain of sand seemed to count down to a future of chaos. The moment's serenity was a thin veil over upcoming trials, set to test Matt's spirit.

His journey was a testament to resilience in a landscape reshaped by fate.

As the wind whispered foreboding messages, Matt's story was about to unfold—a tale of endurance and survival, where each step was a dance with danger, each breath a defiance of death. This was his world, irrevocably altered, demanding resilience as enduring as the desert itself.

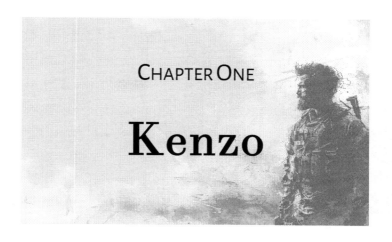

CHAPTER ONE

Kenzo

Some nights, if he was lucky, he'd close his eyes and have a dreamless sleep. He would be met with the darkness of the room that existed just beyond his eyelids. That was what he would hope for every night. But, most nights, he wasn't so lucky. Most nights, he was a victim of his PTSD, thrown into his past and met with the onslaught of reliving a life he had hoped to be redeemed of.

Matt had now found himself on the other side of military life. It was funny to him because it seemed like a lifetime ago, something that was a smudge in the distant and closed recesses of his mind. And yet, he couldn't escape the grasp it held so firmly on his subconscious; couldn't let go of that way of life, of what it had instilled in him.

That day, he was awoken with the sound of chopper blades overhead, sending up tufts of dust from the sandbox in which he spent his days. He was there, in the thick of his hours of active duty, a soldier in the 101st Airborne Division.

"Groover, get yourself over here. You're needed. Now!" Matt suited up and stepped outside. The heat penetrated the dry and arid land, the sand cast phantom figures—tufts sent up into the air. The sun was beating down on him, the stench of five-day-old sweat filled his nose. "Insurgents sighted just east of Baghdad. Get ready, people, this is gonna get ugly."

He eyed his partner in crime, Kenzo Winter. "Keep your wits about you, Ken," he said. "These bastards are sneaky."

"You worry about your own head, Matt," Kenzo shot back, slamming a magazine into his rifle. "Time to show these Hajji fucks we're not here to play games."

They had heard the word "ambush" whispered in hushed tones, so, naturally, everyone was on edge—waiting, anticipating. The platoon that went out the day prior had suffered losses, too many to be acceptable. Matt wasn't about to be yet another name on a growing list of those who would not make it home.

With quick finesse, Matt entered the Humvee and found his way to his position, the most vulnerable yet powerful position in the vehicle—at the top controlling the mounted .50 cal machine gun. He was ready to go, ready to do what was necessary.

Those moments, the ones before they mobilized, were when Matt felt the calm before the storm. All emotion evaporated from his body, as if the human part of him had become robotized somehow. He became a killing machine, thinking only of destruction.

There was silence. It was an eerie calm, just before the chaos ensued. In those moments, all cares and considerations for his mortality seemed to fizzle away. He embodied the immortal beast he knew he was when he had his hands on the .50 cal. He didn't care about his life, but he'd fuck up any son of a bitch who laid a hand on any of his brothers in arms.

They moved across the desert like a herd, the wheels churning up dust all around them, almost as if they were being carried on a cloud.

"We're approaching the location," his sergeant cried. "Everybody be on high alert. They could be anywhere."

Within a split second, the first shot was fired. Misdirected and unguided, the bullet clanked off the side of the humvee, a few inches from Matt's throne. That was when his unit unleashed their shots, aiming at the remains of homes that had been vacated weeks before.

Bullets rained down in quick succession all around him as he unleashed hell. The blaring sound left his ears ringing, drowning out the sound of his racing heartbeat. What had seemed like a routine check regarding a rumored ambush descended into utter and complete chaos when they realized just how many people they were up against.

Beyond the initial structures, there were buildings occupying a three-mile radius. They were like hens in a coop, surrounded by hungry foxes.

"Rain fire on these mother fuckers!" the sergeant roared. Matt didn't need a second invitation.

The power of the .50 cal caused his entire body to vibrate, and his diaphragm echoed with the intense impact as the bullets were violently expelled, each shell casing, flaming hot, landing with an excruciatingly loud and high pitched *clink* that seemed out of place in the violent bass of gunfire. The shells flew around him, some landing on his arms and stinging him with burns that he knew he would never remember. All that mattered was the annihilation of the enemy and the protection of his unit.

He watched as each bullet connected with a target, demolishing bodies, limbs blown into smithereens, replaced with nothing but pink clouds. Matt didn't even recognize the humanity of the enemy. They seemed disposable, because as soon as one was taken out, they were replaced with three more.

He was pulled out of his own mind, ripped from autopilot mode. That was when he became entirely aware of the magnitude of the ambush. He watched bodies collapse around him and became aware of the Apache air support as it unleashed its 30 mm M789

High Explosive Dual Purpose (HEDP) ammunition mercilessly.

He looked around, taking in the body count, all the while maintaining control of his .50 cal.

"Keep them pinned down, Ken!" he yelled at his partner. "We've got these damn bastards on the run!"

From the corner of his eye he spotted Ismail al-Rashid standing behind a human shield of desperate insurgents. The guy was the leader of the local AQI (Al Qhaeda in Iraq) unit and was a force to be reckoned with. His green eyes contrasted against his lean face that had seen years beneath the sun, and when they made contact with Matt, the man gave him a soulless, predator-like grin.

Ismail was a man of power, having served as a sergeant in the Iraqi army. Now, he was a dedicated AQI operative under the command of Abu Musab al-Zarqawi. He was known by the locals as "The Wind," able to disappear with the breeze as swiftly as a zephyr. Until now, he had been untouchable.

Without thought or skipping a beat, Matt pivoted, turning his fire toward the direction of Ismail. He took down two of Ismail's guards, mowing them down like paper, but somehow Ishmel evaded the gunfire, slipping down an alleyway before Matt had the chance to reload.

"Shit! Motherfucker!"

"Fuck!" Kenzo cried. He was on the ground next to the Humvee, blood pouring from a wound in his side. "I'm hit!"

"Don, cover me!" Matt yelled as he moved from his position, sliding down the side of the Humvee. He stumbled his way to Kenzo's side, ripping the material from his pants and holding it to the wound, trying to slow down the stream of blood from leaving Kenzo's body. "No, no! You stay with me, Ken. Stay with me!"

"I got four of them," Kenzo replied, blood bubbling at his lips. "Make sure you notch those up...for me. Don't let Don...claim them."

Bullets slammed into the ground around them, and Matt dragged Ken to the rear of the Humvee. The pain was etched into his pal's face like a deep, jagged scar.

"We're going to get you outta here," Matt cried. "Just you wait and see. Help's on the way. Medic! Medic!"

"Give these to...Stacey." Ken directed, pulling his dog tags from around his neck and handing them to Matt.

"No, Ken, I don't need to—"

"Just...do it. Please." Matt took them in his hand, blood smeared across their metallic surface. "Tell her I...love her."

Matt watched as the life left his pal like smoke, his eyes rolling upward as his head lolled to the side. He clutched the dog tags in his fist and thought of Kenzo's wife. She'd just given birth to his son. *Those bastards, those goddamn sons of bitches. They would be made to pay.*

Just then, he heard loud shouts. But, beyond the mental and emotional turmoil he was feeling, he couldn't make sense of the words that were being screamed. A grenade with the pin missing landed, almost silently, in the desert sand, just 10 feet away from him.

Before he could respond or even register what was happening, the explosion sounded.

Boom!

He expected to be met with a violent, searing pain as his limbs were ripped from his body. He even expected to be met with absolute blackness, knowing that his life had ended. But, instead, he was confronted with something entirely different—his awakening, as he sat bolt upright in bed.

CHAPTER TWO

Family Values

The sweat dripped down his forehead and drenched the bed around him. His breathing was heavy and labored, as if the thick desert air was still surrounding his suburban U.S. home. He sat there for a few seconds, trying to make sense of what had just happened. *There was no way a dream could be that real, could it?*

He thought that, by now, he would have grown accustomed to the onslaught of vivid memories that he was forced to relive almost every night. But still, his heart pounded in his chest, trying desperately to break free from the confines of his rib cage.

Being forced to relive the loss and the heartache seemed too much for him, but the pain and anxiety kept its grasp on his lungs, reminding him of his turmoil. He sat there, trying to hone in his breathing, listening to the clock *tick, tick, tick* away. He was waiting for a release, a single moment of solitude, but it never came.

He dragged himself out of bed and came face-to-face with himself in the bathroom mirror. He was a tall guy at six-foot-three, broad across the shoulders, and he'd always been confident. The war hadn't taken that from him. If anything, it has enhanced it. He knew what he was because of that experience; and while he didn't always like himself, it had given him direction and a purpose.

He stood tall in front of his small bathroom mirror, towering over the sink, with his broad shoulders extending far beyond the confines of the mirror in front of him. His abs, although not as prominent as when he first arrived home from active duty, were clearly defined. When he was in Iraq, working out had been a daily chore. That chore became one of the things that kept him sane when he was home, keeping him focused. He looked at his face in the mirror's reflection. His beard had grown longer than it had ever been before. To think, when he enlisted, his young face could barely cling to stubble.

Matt had always thought of himself as attractive in a rugged way, but what really separated him from those around him was his ability to lead. He'd never found it difficult to tell people what to do; it was just something inside him, a distinct part of his DNA that made him who he was. He'd gone to hell and back in Iraq, but his leadership skills had got him through, even when the shit, quite literally, hit the fan. However, he couldn't escape the possibility that if he had reacted sooner, if he hadn't been so distracted by Ismael al-Rashid, Kenzo would still be alive. *Maybe*.

"Get a hold of yourself, man," he growled. "It was just a dream."

He splashed ice-cold water on his face and tried to focus. It took more time than he cared to admit to get himself back to a stable point, but it was all for nothing. It wasn't long before he was back in bed and haunted by memories of Stacey and her reaction when he saw her for the first time.

He and Kenzo hadn't known each other before Iraq, but they became good friends. And as with most platoons, it wasn't long before they considered each other brothers, ready to lay their lives down for each other without a second thought. Kenzo had told Matt about his girl back home and how they had found out she was pregnant just before he left.

"I'm gonna do right by her, ask her to marry me as soon as we get out of the sandbox," he had said.

"You'd better, boy, or else I'm gonna step in there and steal her from right under your nose. She's a real looker, that one."

"I will bust your southern ass, you sonofabitch!" Kenzo laughed before tossing a bottle at him.

One thing Matt had learned in war is that you would do anything to stay tethered to a reality that wasn't riddled with death and violence. For Kenzo, his tether was Stacey. She represented everything good and pure that war tried to erase from his life. This meant that Matt had come to know so much about her, even though he never met her.

When they lost Kenzo, Matt was torn apart, knowing that his friend would never get to meet his kid.

He knew that all Stacey and her son would ever have of Kenzo was a neatly folded flag, and that just didn't seem like enough.

When he came back from active duty, he fought the urge to call her, but he found resolve in knowing that it would make his friend happy. They met for drinks at a bar in the town where she and her son lived. The conversation started out with the usual pleasantries, and it progressed gradually. Matt had taken it upon himself to assure her that she and her son, Kenzo Jr, would always be taken care of.

"He loved you. You know that, right?" he'd asked her, sipping a bourbon on ice.

"Yeah, I do."

"Spoke about you all the time. Showed me all the photographs."

"Only the good ones, I hope."

"Oh, they were all good, believe me," Matt said, smiling.

They'd bonded over their grief, and that was probably what pushed them over the edge, wanting to feel that connection again—that emotional bond. Since that moment, he'd tried to talk himself into believing he had been thinking of Kenzo—that he'd been trying to do the right thing—but there was no way he could justify what happened next. He and Stacey had ended up in bed together that night, and even though his initial intentions had been pure, he could not wash the guilt away. They never spoke again.

He lay there in his bed, tormented by the demons of his past, wondering if he'd ever find freedom from the chains that bound him so tightly. Maybe he was the devil himself. He was terrified to close his eyes again, terrified of what he might see the next time he drifted off to sleep.

Once again, he was back in Iraq, moving through the streets, Kenzo's blood still on his hands. *The bastard had to suffer, he had to be taken out.* The others in his platoon followed him, moving from building to building, ushering civilians out and shooting anybody who posed a threat. Kenzo's dog tags were tucked into his belt, his friend's final words playing on repeat in his head.

"Over there," one of the men cried. "I saw him. He just went into that building. He's with three guards."

Matt drove them forward, crouching low, their weapons trained on the windows, waiting for their enemy to show themselves.

"Two of us will take the rear entrance," he said. "The other two, take the front." There was a spray of bullets on the ground ahead of them and they returned fire, taking out one of the guards who fell backward into the room, remnants of his skull decorating the building's exterior. "Now!" Matt cried, and they breached the door, taking out another guard before mounting the stairs two at a time. "Guns down, hands on your heads!" he yelled. "Put your fucking guns down!"

He had him. Ismael al-Rashid was cornered like a rat. The anticipation burned hot on his skin. *He would avenge Kenzo. He would do it for his brother.*

The door before him exploded in a hail of wood and bullets, and his buddy, Iniesto, took one in the hand.

"Goddamn it!" he yelled.

Matt leaped to the edge of the doorway, his heart pounding in his chest. He'd been too cocky, expecting al-Rashid to simply lay down his arms. He pulled the pin on the flash grenade and tossed it into the room.

The noise was deafening, but he didn't hesitate. He moved in, opening up on the guard. The Iraqi fell to the ground, his body peppered with bullets.

Ismael was making his escape through an open window.

"Stop right there, al-Rashid!" Matt cried. "You make one goddamn move, and I'll blow your fucking brains out."

The AQI lieutenant turned to him, his lips curled in a hateful sneer. "Do as you will, infidel. My soul is clean. Can you say the same about yours?"

He moved, reaching a hand into his robe, but Matt reacted first. He pulled the trigger, putting three bullets in al-Rashid's chest, throwing him out the window and onto the roof below.

Matt rushed to the opening and looked down. Al-Rashid's eyes peered up at him, looking like nothing more than lifeless black orbs. His hand was gripping a photograph of a woman and young child.

Matt opened his own eyes and glared at his bedroom ceiling. They'd called him a hero after that one kill. It had always seemed absurd to him. He'd killed so many, and yet that one moment, the time where he'd acted on pure instinct, driven by the desire to avenge his dead pal, had been hailed as heroic and awe-inspiring.

He'd been given the Silver Star, something that still felt surreal to him. His friend lay in his grave, his family cursed to live the rest of their lives without him, and yet Matt was being celebrated? When he'd returned home he'd tossed the medal in a drawer and never looked at it again. He'd betrayed Kenzo, which meant he'd also betrayed himself.

He'd headed straight for his mom's house on that first day back. He never forgot walking up the patio steps to the front door with his buzz cut, still in his uniform, knowing that for a while, at least, he could enjoy normality as well as his mom's world famous cobbler. However, when his momma opened the front door, his jaw dropped. She looked so gaunt and frail.

"Hi, Mom."

"Matthew? You're home."

"Yeah, for a while, at least." He smiled. "Guess they wanted to get me outta their hair for a couple weeks.

Is he here?" Matt asked, referring to his father, a guy he still had nightmares about.

She shook her head, her eyes anxiously scanning the street. "He's out. Be back in a while."

"O'Flannigan's?" It was his dad's favorite haunt, after all.

She avoided the question. "You want some coffee? I just brewed a pot."

"Thought you'd never ask."

They sat at the kitchen counter, sipping the hot, bitter liquid, reminiscing about old times and talking about his aunts and uncles. His father's name was never mentioned, as it was a topic that neither of them wanted to broach.

"You been okay, Mom?" he asked. "You've lost a lot of weight."

"Your dad lost his job, so we've been cutting back."

He wanted to say, "*But that bastard can still afford to get blind drunk in the middle of the afternoon? Same as always*," but he knew the vitriol wouldn't help.

"You can cut back, Mom, but you still gotta eat."

"Don't you worry about me, son. I am eating. I eat plenty. I needed to drop a few pounds anyway."

He shook his head, wincing at the sight of his mom's jawbone through her thin skin, and reached for his wallet. "Here, I've been saving for a rainy day, but the thing is, it never rains in the desert."

"No!" she bit back, pushing the thick cluster of bills away. "We don't need it."

"It's not for him. It's for you!"

Her face went pale, her lips trembled. "We don't want your money, Matthew. We don't!"

"You mean, you're afraid of what he'll do to you when he finds out! You don't have to worry about him, Mom. Not anymore."

"He's your father!"

"He left you, Mom. Split from you when I was a kid. He only came back because he needed money. And he hit me every day, too, until I was big enough to stand up for myself. He's no father of mine!"

"He's my husband!" She hollered, shaking as the tears started to come.

"And this is how he treats you? Leaving you at home with no food while he wastes what little money you have down at the bar."

She turned and headed to the window, glaring at the street below. "We made our vows in front of God, and that still means something."

Matt went to her then, turning her toward him. "And God would not want one of his children to be treated this way!"

The house felt like it was closing in on him, as though, any second, his father would come barrelling through the door, a belt in his hands, his eyes red with the vacant whiskey stare.

"I think it's best you go," she said, those six words that still felt like daggers in his heart. "He'll be home soon and...well, you know?"

He staggered down the street, emotional and confused. This wasn't the homecoming he'd expected, or the life he'd wanted. He loved his mom, but she was so blinded by love that she could barely see what was going on.

He headed to O'Flannigan's on autopilot, almost without thinking. He had to make things right, do something at least. There were three guys standing in the parking lot, smoking Chesterfields and chugging on beer. He stood some distance away, trying to make out if one of them was his old man, but none of them looked old enough.

He headed for the big green door, which had seen better days, and that was when he saw him. He was a little older, less hair on his head, and his face had the yellow sheen of liver disease and cigarette smoke. His dad almost passed him by before he shot him a sideways glance through bloodshot eyes that were half-closed.

"Matthew?" he growled, his voice soaked in bourbon. "Is that you?"

Matt suckerpunched him, knocking him against the wall where he slumped to the ground.

"Holy shit, boy. What you go and do that for?" he asked, his voice groggy as his trembling hand rubbed his jaw furiously.

"You okay, Ray?" one of the smokers asked, edging toward Matt.

"Yeah, I'm fine. This here's my son."

"Does he always greet you like that?" one of the other guys sneered.

"Only when he's in a bad mood."

A police car went by, its siren wailing, and the three men hastily dispersed.

"Went to see Mom," Matt hissed. "She don't look so good."

"What you talking 'bout? She's fine." His father drew out the last syllable.

"Says you got no money on account of you losing your job...again!"

His dad hauled himself unsteadily to his feet. "Things ain't been the same since I left the force. I'm just going through a rough patch is all. It'll end soon enough."

"Not if you keep drinking away everything you have."

His father eyed the bar, his lips moist. Matt could see he was craving the comfort of the establishment's subtle lighting, coupled with its solitude. "Just came down for a beer or two. Nothing wrong with that."

"Except a beer or two becomes seven or eight, and then you chase those down with four double bourbons and a whiskey sour." He said as he stepped toward him, their faces so close together they were almost touching. "Here, take this."

His father eyes the wad of cash. "What? I don't want that!"

"She won't take it because she's afraid of you, but I won't see my mother wasting away because my lowlife dad can't take care of her."

"You should watch your mouth, son."

"I did that my whole childhood, Dad. I'm not a kid anymore."

"I can still whip your scrawny little ass."

"Take the money, and put it to good use."

"I can look after myself, thanks."

Matt grabbed his father's shirt collar and pushed him backward. He could smell the whiskey on his breath and the nicotine on his skin. "You take it, and you look after my mom. If I find out you're spending it here, or anywhere like this, I'll come back and, I swear to God, I'll kill you."

His father's stern demeanor seemed to shift just a little, and he looked at the money once more. "What am I even supposed to do with it?"

"Buy food, pay the heating bill, decorate the place. I don't care. Just don't blow it on alcohol or at the poker table."

They stood that way for a little while, his father looking like a shell of the police officer he once was, and Matt now four times the kid he had once been. The power dynamics had shifted, and his dad knew it.

"I can't promise anything," he said.

"You try real hard, Dad, because I mean it. I'll be back, and this time, I'll make damn sure you pay."

He turned his back and walked away, feeling like something had shifted inside him. Matt never looked back at his father, but he knew he watched his son the whole way, wondering what the hell had just happened.

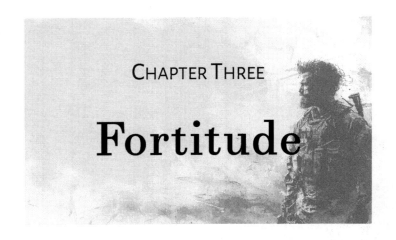

CHAPTER THREE

Fortitude

After a few weeks of living in a hotel and keeping an eye on his parents' place, Matt was shipped back out to sandbox, feeling as satisfied as he could that his dad was going to do as he was told. He was also a couple of pounds heavier from eating junk food and watching TV. *Life as a civilian wasn't as entertaining as it was cracked up to be.*

It took him a while to get back into the swing of things. The workouts seemed harder and the training seemed more grueling, but it wasn't long before he hit his stride. He was a soldier, after all. Being back with his platoon was like being back with his brothers.

Three weeks after landing back in Iraq, he was sitting with a bunch of guys, talking about the day's excursions. They all sat around him as he reclined atop the Humvee, greasing his treasured .50 cal. That gun had saved both him and his pals more times than he cared to think about.

They were talking about something dumb and laughing, which was a normal routine. Humor kept them all sane. In the distance, they saw their first shirt and lieutenant, Jerry Michaelson, walking over.

"No need to stop on my account, gentlemen," he said to everyone as the tone became more serious. "I'm just here for Matthew."

"Everything alright, Lieutenant?" Matt asked, not knowing what it could be about.

"Everything's fine. The commander wants to see you."

He looked around at his boys, wondering what was going on. He knew he would be in for some jokes at his expense later for gaining an audience with their senior officer. Some of them already called him the lieutenant's favorite. This was only going to make matters worse, but it was okay. He was a big boy and could give as good as he got.

He jumped from the top of the humvee, his boots making contact with the sand with a muffled *thump*. His tags knocked against each other and the sound seemed to resonate in his ears. Immediately, his mind began racing as he took a detailed tally of everything that had happened over the past three days. He went over every kill, every shot fired, and every command followed.

Did I kill an innocent bystander? Did I not follow commands? What could I have done? I must be in trouble. I've fucked around before, but this is way too formal to be nothing, he thought.

Just before they entered the commander's tent, the lieutenant stopped him. "You packing?" Lieutenant Jerry asked.

"Always, as I should be."

"I'm gonna need you to disarm."

"Yes sir."

Matt handed over his handgun, wondering what the hell was going on. *What could be so bad that the lieutenant felt the need to take away anything that could harm someone?* Matt wasn't dangerous to his own side. He'd proven that in theater.

The last weapon to be removed was his Gerber Mk2 Combat Knife, which was strapped to his right calf. All of it was piled in his lieutenant's arms before he built up the courage to ask, "How bad is it?"

Lieutenant Jerry just nudged his head sideward.

He walked into a solemn space. Every possible thought ran through his mind as he made his way toward his commander, who was sitting at a makeshift table with a few files in front of him. Standing next to the commander was the on-duty medic, who slowly nodded his greeting to Matt.

"That's the thing about war, soldier," the commander said, as if they had been having this conversation long before he even walked in. "The paperwork never ends. Have a seat, Matt." His commander gestured for him to sit down, but Matt caught the glance that he gave Jerry.

"Thanks, Commander."

"How you doing, Matt? You okay?"

"I'm fine, sir. Uh, may I ask what's goin' on? Is everything alright? Has there been a report about me?"

"No, no, nothing like that. Um, I'm gonna be honest here. I'm a man who is rarely without words, but right now, I kind of don't know what to say. I've given a lot of bad news to families about the men we've lost here, but I have never had to do this the other way around. Matt, it's your mom. Your brother found her unconscious in the family home this morning."

"I—I'm sorry, Commander, I—I don't think I follow," The words were a jumble to Matt, like a puzzle that has yet to be solved.

"I'm told they did everything they could. She fought a good fight, but I'm afraid she passed a little after noon."

"*What?!* But she was fine when I last saw her—a little thin maybe. There were dark patches around her eyes, but—" His sentence trailed off, unfinished. He was talking to himself, trying to piece together what he was hearing while attempting to make sense of this news.

"I'm sorry, Matt."

Silence.

Lieutenant Jerry put his hand on his shoulder.

Silence.

"How could this have happened?"

"They think there was an intruder. Some things were broken in the house, the door had been kicked in, and your mother—" the commander paused. "She sustained some head injuries, seemingly from an attack with a blunt object."

Matt had a moment of intense clarity, almost as if someone was projecting a movie on the commander's wall in 4K, ultra high definition. He saw *him* holding a belt, swinging at his son's head moments before he swigged yet another bourbon—*him* being none other than the old man staggering from O'Flannigan's.

You should watch your mouth, son.

I can still whip your scrawny little ass.

I can't promise anything.

"That motherfucker!"

Everything moved way too fast. He started to feel rage building up, the anger burning at his temples. *He would kill him. He would kill the sick sonofabitch. He would beat him into a pulp until all that was left was a tangled mess of blood and bone.*

"Soldier, I know this is horrible news, but please try to control yourself."

"I need to go home. I need to get outta here!"

"And you will—soon. But, for now, we need you here."

"No!" Matt yelled, knocking files from his commanding officer's desk. "Now! I need to go now!"

The medic was on top of him, and he felt the hot sting of a needle in his thigh.

Silence.

He woke up more than 24 hours later, groggy, disorientated, and shattered all over again. The image of his mom's face—dejected and lost—painted his senses. *How could he? How could his own father do such a thing?*

It wasn't until much later, when he spoke to the guys, that they told him about the piercing screams that reverberated through the thick desert air, screams that never abated until the sedative took effect, screams that he never heard—screams that were drowned out by the pain.

By the time he arrived back home, his father, an ex-police officer who had once been the shining light of the local force, had been taken into custody. The evidence was irrefutable. His bloodied fingerprints on the doorframe, along with his hammer lying beside his wife's fractured skull. There had been a large amount of alcohol in his bloodstream, enough to render a man of casual intake unconscious. However, his father's intake was anything but casual. He was an addict, living every moment of every day for his next hit, his next high.

Matt went to see his mother as she laid in an open casket. The undertaker had carried out meticulous repairs. He could barely see the fractures in his mom's skull or the deep indentation behind her ear. She seemed at peace, perhaps for the first time in decades—maybe even since she met her husband.

"I'm sorry, Mom," he apologized, thinking about the money he had handed his father and how he had abused Matt's trust. "I thought I could change him. I was wrong. I'm so, so sorry."

He broke down, gripping his mother's cold lifeless hand, wanting her back there standing beside him and consoling him. He had inadvertently caused his mother's death and that one tragic epiphany would live with him forever. *Good deeds, it seemed, were a fool's errand. Better to look out for yourself and let everyone else deal with their own shit.* He knew that now.

For a few weeks, he floated around aimlessly, haunted by his own mind and dark thoughts. His tours were done, his military life now in his rear view mirror, and it left him feeling like a soul out of place, a man without a center.

After a month, he got his own place, furnished with nothing but a mattress and a TV. He had slowly begun isolating himself from his family, his brother, and everyone else around him. After all, he wasn't the same person he was before he had been deployed, and he convinced himself that no one needed this new and forever-changed version of him in their life. His father's face haunted his every waking thought, and he saw his image every time he looked at his brother or stared at his own reflection. He just couldn't escape it.

It was the month of his brother Marshall's birthday, and he was invited over. The family was having some sort of gathering. The thought of attending the event filled him with anxiety, but he got dressed, poured himself a double Jack to ease the gnawing feeling in his chest, and steeled himself. As he got to his apartment door, hand on the knob, he stopped. Something was standing in his way and he couldn't quite figure out what it was. He went back into the kitchen, grabbed a flask from the cabinet, and filled it to the brim with Jack Daniels. He had a feeling he was going to need it.

He arrived at his brother's four-bedroom home with a rolling front lawn, and suddenly his pulse started to race. The driveway was stacked four deep with dozens of cars.

Holy fuck, he thought, *the whole neighborhood and then some is here.*

Before he got out of his truck, he took out his flask and took another swig of his liquid courage. "Shit," he said to himself. "I don't need this."

He greeted everyone with a smile as his brother walked him around. He hugged aunts, uncles, cousins, and neighbors. He embraced people he had never met, and cringed at the word "hero," which is what he had miraculously come to be known as. Even his fifth-grade teacher, Mr Ellis, the one who had said he "would never amount to nothin'," gave him an attaboy and a slap on the back.

It was loathsome. He hated every second of it but sought desperately to appease his brother. He looked at the people who celebrated him, celebrated his actions, but they knew absolutely nothing about what he had done. They congratulated him and called him a "blessing to his country," but he didn't feel like one. Heroism was for sycophants. He'd tried to be a hero for his mom, and look where that had gotten him.

"Matt. Matt!" his brother called. "Ya stuck in yer head there, boy?"

"Ha, yeah, it's been happening a lot. The scare of war, and all that."

His brother took his arm and led him onto the back porch. "Look, I wanted to talk to you about something."

Matt didn't like his brother's tone, but the whiskey had worked its magic and he stood there, peering at him through a foggy haze.

"It's about Dad."

Matt felt a burning pain in his gut. "I don't have a dad."

"I know. I really do. I know exactly how you feel, and I agree with you."

"Do you?"

"Yeah. What?! Of course, I do. Jesus, Matt. She was my mother too, you know?"

Those words were like hot stones, stark and scalding.

"He's an addict, Matt, pure and simple. He did what he did because of the booze. If he had been sober, who knows how things might have turned out."

"He had a choice to make, and he chose liquor. He could have chosen sobriety, but he didn't."

Marshall eyed the tumbler of whiskey in Matt's hand. "Fortitude is hard to come by, Matt. What is it that Father Ferguson used to say? *"Because the Lord helps me, I will not be disgraced. Therefore, have I set*

my face like flint, and I know I will not be put to sha
me.""

"Don't quote the bible to me, Marshall. I know
what it says."

"Then, you'll know that our dad needs help, Matt,
not an exorcism."

"He needs the needle, that's what he needs—and
even that's too good for him." Matt hissed.

His words seemed to stun his brother into silence.
They stood there, glaring at each other, not knowing
what to say. Matt needed another drink, but he was
too aware that he was being judged.

"A visit wouldn't hurt, you know?" Marshall said
after a moment.

"You visit then."

"I already have."

"You what?" Matt almost dropped his glass. He
couldn't believe what he was hearing.

"I went with Cindy a couple of weeks ago. You were
settling into your new place, and I didn't want to
disturb you."

"You didn't think this was important?"

"Yeah, sure, but I also knew you'd be against it."

"Hell yeah. No shit!" Matt's blood was boiling. *How dare he do this. How dare he!*

"He wants to see you."

"He can rot in hell."

"And he probably will, but he still wants to see his eldest son one last time."

Matt downed the last of his drink and tossed the glass. "I want nothing to do with him. If he wasn't in that cell, I'd kill him with my own bare hands."

"You're not serious."

"I've never been more serious about anything in my entire life."

Marshall glanced over his shoulder toward the party. It was starting to get going, the music and chit-chat increasing in volume, coupled by sporadic, loud laughter. It all seemed like such a juxtaposition to their tense conversation.

"He said he has something he needs to tell you. Something you would want to hear."

"I'm done with this conversation," Matt sniped, turning his back.

"It's about Mom. She told Dad something, something important, and he wants you to hear it from him."

Matt's heart dropped. *His mom.* They'd parted on such shitty terms. Maybe she wanted to make amends. Perhaps she didn't blame him.

"This had better be good, brother," he said, leaving Marshall standing alone. "This had better be damn good."

CHAPTER FOUR

Spitballing

"Groover!" one of the guards yelled.

Matt watched from his place at the table as his father entered. He was dressed in a yellow jumpsuit that looked at least a size too big for him. He looked every one of his sixty-two years, his hair thin and gray, the creases around his eyes and mouth deep and plentiful. The skin at his neck sagged like old leather and his cheeks were sallow. Matt fought the urge to stand up and launch himself at him. He just couldn't shift the image of his father raining hammer blows down on his petite mother's skull.

"Son," his dad said as he sat down.

"I don't want to be here."

"And yet, here you are."

Matt's heart was pounding in his chest. He had fought dozens of battles in Iraq against a foe he could barely comprehend, but this was something else entirely. He didn't know what to do or say; he just wanted to get up and run.

"Why did you do it?" he asked, surprising himself as the words escaped his lips.

"I don't know. I don't remember."

"Your lawyer says you're trying to claim diminished responsibility. You know that's bullshit, right?"

"I didn't know what I was doing, son. You have to believe me."

"The only thing I believe is that you got so wasted on the money you should have been spending on her, that you took out your self-loathing and regret on my mother—the one woman who would have done anything for you."

"If I did, I didn't mean to."

"But you did just the same."

His father's head dropped. "Yeah, I know. You're right."

His admission shocked Matt into silence. "Just take your poison. Plead guilty and do your time."

"That means I'll die in here."

"If that's what the judge decides."

His father shook his head. "I don't know if I can do that."

Matt gripped the edge of the table, his knuckles white. "You don't have a choice, just like Mom didn't choose to be killed by her husband, you worthless piece of sh—" He stopped himself, realizing the guard was taking an interest in their exchange. Matt took a moment to compose himself and quickly changed tack. "Marshall said you had something to tell me."

His dad nodded. "Guess I do."

"Well, either you do or you don't. Either way, I'll be outta here in a little while and you'll never see me again."

"Don't be like that, kid. I raised you, didn't I?"

"If you mean kicked the shit outta me on a regular basis, locked me in the closet for hours at a time, and broke pretty much everything I ever owned, then I guess, yeah, you did."

His dad shrugged. "I never claimed to be father of the year."

"That's good. Because you weren't. Far from it."

"Taught you how to fish, though, didn't I? Took you to church every week. Showed you how to shoot straight."

Matt slammed his hand on the table, causing the other visitors to glance in their direction. The guard stepped toward their table.

"Everything okay here?" he asked.

"Yeah, fine," Matt replied, averting his gaze. "We're just spitballing, that's all."

"Okay, then. Appreciate it if you could keep the noise down. There's other visits going on."

"Got it, sir. You'll get no more trouble from us," Matt said, wincing as he tried to calm himself. When the guard departed, he turned back to his father. "Those trips to the lake, to the gun range, they always ended up back at the bar with you barely able to walk and me nursing a black eye or split lip."

His dad's lips curled upward. "We had some good times, boy. You just choose to forget."

"I remember every damn second, but it's not by choice." He went to stand. "Look, if you have nothing real to say, I'm gone. Enjoy the rest of your life in here, Dad. Hope it was worth it."

"Wait!" his father said, reaching for him. "Wait a second."

Matt glared at him.

"She never told you. I asked her to, many times, but I guess she couldn't bring herself to do it. Even after I left her, she refused to reveal the truth. We tried, you see. Over and over again, for months, but nothing happened. At first, we thought it was her. Then, God forbid, we thought it might be me. We went to the doctor, we prayed every night, but still, every month the same—blood in her panties and a drawer full of tiny clothes we would never use."

"What?" Matt sat down. "What the hell are you saying?"

"We knew a family, drug addicts with barely a dollar to their name. They needed money, and we knew they couldn't care for their kid. No way. They could barely look after themselves. We struck up a deal, a private one—no fancy lawyers, no courts—and your mom wore a fat suit for a while—made it look like the real thing. Before too long, we did the exchange and, after that, we were just as happy as pigs in mud."

"You adopted a child?"

"You could put it like that, only less official. Except, after a few months, the woman came knocking, wanting more money. We'd just about spent everything we had on the initial deal and had nothing left to give. The dad? Well, he'd upped and left weeks before, taking the remaining cash and left the woman with nothing, and she needed her next high like the devil needs lost souls.

"Anyway, we gave her what little money we had left from a pot we kept above the stove, but that wasn't enough. A week later, she was back, threatening us with the cops. I couldn't have that, what with me being on the force and all. Your mom was a mess, barely sleeping, and I was working nights, trying to scramble together enough dough to keep a roof over our heads. We had to do something."

"She took the kid, didn't she?" Matt sniped. "That's why you're telling me this. I suppose it hurt so bad that it drove you to drink, and that's why you treated us so badly. You're trying to make me feel sorry for you, aren't you?"

His father shook his head, looking for something in his hands that wasn't there. "We'd never have given that child up, not then. We didn't know if we could ever have kids of our own, and for all we knew, that was our only shot of having a family."

"So, what then? You just ignored her until she went away? You paid her some more money?"

His father's face had turned a sickening gray, and he glared at the tips of his fingers. "You have no clue that you can kill someone until you actually do, you know? You must know that. You've killed plenty, I'm sure. I was in my early 30s, I'd barely seen or done anything. Didn't even drink much back then. But that night, when that woman was in our home, screaming at us—saying evil, nasty things—I just snapped."

"You mean—"

His father's voice became a hushed whisper. "Your mother helped me hide the body in the basement. I dug a hole, filled it in with concrete. She's still there as far as I know."

Matt eyed the guards. "You killed her?"

"Of course, we didn't know then that we would have another son a year later; but this time, a natural birth, our baby, not from some crack addict and his skank of a wife. A son we could truly love. The problem was, that image in my head never went away—of the life being choked out of her—and every time I looked at her kid, that was all I saw. The agony, the terror, the hatred."

Matt didn't know what to think, didn't know what to feel. He now knew his father had killed two people, not just his own mother, and yet he'd tossed the words from his mouth as casually as blowing smoke. He tried to compose himself. He had so many questions. "So, what happened when I came along? Did you give the adopted baby away? Did it die? Did the father come back?"

"That's time, people!" the prison guard roared.

"I gotta go," Matt's dad said. "Finish this next time?"

"But, the baby?" Matt demanded. "I have to know!"

As the guard took hold of his father's arms and marched him away, the old man stopped to look once more at his son, a leering grin on his face—the one that used to appear when he was bearing down on Matt, reeking of bourbon, with the buckle of his belt swinging loosely in his hand.

"Look in the mirror," he spat. "You'll find your answer there."

CHAPTER FIVE

Power Play

The events of the weekend kept echoing through his mind. *His parents weren't his real parents at all.* He had two mothers, both of whom had been murdered by the man he once thought of as his father, but he wasn't really his father—or at least that's what he'd implied. His own father, his real flesh and blood dad, had abandoned him for the price of a few dollar bills and some blow. Everything was such a mess, and on top of that, he'd lost his best pal in Iraq and he'd done the unthinkable by screwing the man's wife. *If anyone was the fuck up here, it was him, and was it any wonder?*

He felt a darkness within him. It was slowly beginning to spread—like a splatter of black ink left on the canvas of his life, smeared by war. It was constantly growing, trying to take over him. It had already won his heart and it was making its way to his mind. He could feel it, especially at night when he was alone. His dreams erupted to life in an onslaught of emotion, driven by pain and loss. He would be subjected to the same pain and heartache all over again, never having a moment of relief.

Despite being tormented by demons, his days were empty and devoid of purpose. He knew he needed to do something with his time, take his mind off of everything. He was now a man without a place, a man without direction. He'd come home to bury his mother, but his real mother was buried in his father's basement under a few feet of concrete. He thought about calling it in, but what good would it do? She was long gone, and for all he knew, his dad was just lying, trying to inflict as much emotional damage as possible before his son tossed him out of his life for good.

He could only reach one unfathomable conclusion: People were inherently bad. There was just no getting round that fact.

There was a thought that he had been playing around with, rolling over and over in his mind. Sunday, after the incident with his dad, he made his way to Sailors, the local pub he'd often frequented before heading out for Iraq, and he asked for a guy he once knew.

"Is Mr Winston in?" he asked the bartender.

"You mean old Vic?" the guy asked, wiping a towel over a damp glass.

"That's the guy."

"Yeah, he's out back. I guess he's powdering his nose."

Matt took a bar stool and ordered a Modelo. It was still early in the day, and Marshall's words were still rolling around in his head. *Fortitude is hard to come by, Matt.*

He thought about his colleagues in the platoon, wondering what they were doing at that exact moment. One thing was for sure, they wouldn't be in a warm bar, sitting on a comfortable stool, sipping an ice cold beer. The war shone a bright beam on the ordinary, the mundane, and made those things seem amazing and awesome. It was the art of not having, which made you appreciate what you had.

"Well, as I live and breathe. If it isn't young Matthew Groover?"

Matt turned and watched the rotund man come swaying toward him, the remains of an extinguished cigar clamped between his fingers. He had a round face, glasses perched on the tip of a bulbous nose, and dark, graying hair that hung in loose strands.

Victor Winston had been a friend of his father's before his dad left the force, before he had been fired for showing up at the station drunk one time too many. He reached out and drew Matt in, hugging him.

"I'm so sorry," he said. "I heard the news and—" His voice cracked. "How you holding up? You and your brother keeping it together?"

Matt nodded, thinking about everything that had happened since he'd returned home, but chose to keep those particular facts to himself. He wasn't ready to talk about it yet.

"Yeah, well, you know? It's been tough, but we're keeping it together."

"Well, you're a stronger man than me, I can tell you that." He nodded to the bartender who poured him a Whiskey Mac. "Drink?" he asked, pointing to Matt's semi-consumed bottle.

"No, I'm fine," he replied. "Just came in to catch up with an old friend. Seems like I don't have many of those around here anymore."

"Yes, I'm sure. Your father's always been a troubled man, but this? *Phew!* I didn't see it coming. Perhaps I should have."

Matt glared at his beer. "You can't blame yourself, Victor. The only person who is to blame is doing time, and I'm hoping he does a lot of it."

Mr Winston sipped on his drink and took a deep breath. "So, what you doin' now that you're no longer a soldier? Got anything to keep you occupied?" The question lingered in the air.

"Nothin' as yet, sir. Why? You got something in mind?"

"Funny you say that," he replied, grabbing a handful of nuts and throwing them in his mouth. "Just this morning, the preacher was talking about an idle mind and how it can be the devil's workshop. I ain't ever been in active duty myself, but I had a cousin who was. I know just how much he struggled when he got home. Heck, his mind was the devil's full-time residence, if you ask me. Anyway, if you're interested, we could always use some extra hands on the force. They still got all of us old folk pounding the streets, and with all the bad hips joints, we're struggling to chase our own shadows." He chuckled at his own joke. "So, what do you say? Your experience would be a valuable asset to us, and you've already gained the kind of knowledge that surpasses what the academy could teach."

Matt thought back on the months before he was deployed and how he had considered being an officer, despite the job's connection with his father. He had so much pent up aggression, he needed some way of focusing it.

"Thank you for the offer, Vic. I will definitely consider it."

And that was what Matt was doing, considering it. It wasn't as easy as just showing up at the station and interviewing, at least not to Matt. He'd seen what people did to others, what people like his dad did to his own wife. If he was going to do it, he was going to make a difference—and then some.

Matt and his brother had been marched to church every Sunday and taught the ways of the scripture: about how you should love your fellow man, how you should show compassion and forgiveness, and how you should never hurt another human being. All of that amounted to nothing if your own kin was keeping secrets from you and hurting those you were closest to. It all seemed so futile.

But, now, it was 10:45 on a Wednesday morning, and he was laying on his bed, looking at the ceiling, contemplating his life. He was already at the bottom of two beer bottles and in hot pursuit of the third. He knew that if he lay there any longer, he would have to face up to a few things. A few home truths.

He sat up and swung his feet over the side of the bed, and the decision hit him, almost as if it was decided for him. He was going to do it, he was going to join the force. *What harm could it do, right?* But, he would do it tomorrow. *Yeah*, he thought as he reached for his third beer, *definitely tomorrow.*

He sat upright in his bed, his chest heaving, panting, and sweat dripping all over him. He looked around and saw that it was 3 am—the witching hour. Most people dream about their new job and how terrified they are of messing up their interview. Heck, some "normal" people dream of showing up at work without wearing any pants. He, on the other hand, dreamed of a missile striking the police department, one that was strangely located right in the middle of the sandbox. He should have known that nothing would help him escape the torment of his past.

Still, he lay back down, wondering who the heck he was fooling and prepared himself to drift into a sleep that was plagued with loud noises, screams, and blood. *It never came.*

He lay on his bed, looking at the blank canvas of his apartment. There was nothing homely about it. He could pack up everything he owned at any moment and vanish without leaving a trace behind him. He thought about it. No one would miss him. Marshall had his own life, his own family, and, from what his father had told him, the two of them weren't even related at all. If he put a bullet through his head now, no one would mourn him the way he had mourned his mother.

He gazed into the blackness, thoroughly disturbed by the silence, and for a mere second, he wondered if he missed the havoc of war; the possibility that at any second, you could be awoken by an explosion. The constant discomfort of being on edge, because in an instant, you would need to kill or be killed.

As soon as the thought entered his mind, he was overwhelmed with guilt. He was disgusted at the fact that he missed the sounds of war. It was the very thing that cost humans their lives and had cost him his best friend's life.

He stayed there for hours, berating himself for his pride at being called a "killing machine," happy that he was home safe lying in bed, guilty that he was lying in his bed when others never would. He was cut adrift with no platoon, family, or connection to anything or anyone. The emotions ebbed and flowed, carrying him along on the current of unease and raw emotion. He felt angry at the world, pissed off but fragile too, as if the very fabric of his very existence was being torn apart.

When the alarm sounded it was a welcome release. He had a job to go to.

He was dressed in what he considered his best. He didn't own a button down, so he wore cargo pants and a black t-shirt. After all, he was an army man. Before he left his apartment, he stood in the kitchen, contemplating his next move, and quickly decided that he couldn't do this without some liquid courage.

He pushed the whiskey aside and poured himself a shot of vodka—realizing he couldn't go in, reeking of alcohol. He stood there for a second, feeling the burning sensation slowly making its way down his throat. He looked at the bottle again.

"Fuck it!" he said, taking a gigantic gulp straight from the bottle and wincing as it made its way down to his stomach.

He thought of his so-called father, of what he had done under the influence of one too many bourbons, and he tossed the bottle aside, relishing the fog as it numbed his senses. He threw on his shades and made his way down to the station.

He was greeted with fake smiles and pleasantries. Most of the rookies were guys he went to school with. He knew everyone there, and everyone knew that he had seen some shit. *The joys of living in a small town, I guess*, he thought.

He saw Mr Winston from across the room, and he immediately regretted coming. He sauntered over to where Matt was sitting outside the chief's office.

"I see you came," the old man said.

"Yes sir. Thought I'd stop by, you know. Had some time on my hands."

Mr Winston chuckled. "I like you, young man, always have. Reckon you may actually do something 'round here."

"Well, I'm definitely gonna try. If the chief allows me."

Leroy Mathers was Marshall's age, making him a year or two younger than Matt. He was a knuckle-head, to say the least, and was always pushed aside or left out in high school. With the town being as small as it was, Leroy went straight into the academy after leaving and climbed the ladder pretty quickly. The power he acquired swiftly went to his head, and he exercised it at every opportunity. He walked around like a trigger-happy gunslinger, ready to whip out his badge and gun and exert every bit of authority he could.

He married a local girl named Lori and had two kids, but the rumor was that neither were actually his. Lori had quite the reputation in school, and people had amazing memories when it came to scandal and intrigue. Leroy lived in ignorant bliss of what most people thought, though, apparently never hearing what went on during Lori and her girlfriends' infamous "girls' nights."

"Well, the chief ain't got no damn option," Mr Winston said. "Look, you ain't gonna be doin' half the shit I can only imagine you've done in the past few years. It's a small town. Everyone you're gonna reprimand or arrest is someone you know, or someone whose daddy you know. You're only gonna see familiar faces around here. In some cases, that's harder; but in others, it's easier. Either way, we ain't ever seen much to write home about in these parts—not until your dad did what he did, of course."

Just then, the door opened and three officers walked out, laughing and joking. The thick and heavy smell of fries and fried chicken wafted out of the chief's office, making Matt's stomach growl.

"...You boys better watch it now," the chief hollered from his office, almost choking on his food. "Ah, Matty boy! If it isn't our town's very own war hero? Come on in here, man! How the heck are ya? It's good to see you!"

Matt walked into the office and sat down, wondering who the fuck ate fried chicken at 10 am, but when he saw that the Leroy he once knew was now at least 70 pounds heavier, everything became much clearer. Clearly the guy had been eating his feelings. The once dorky and average-sized man he remembered had been replaced with a sweaty and heavy-breathing slob who stuffed food in his mouth as if living in fear of somebody stealing it.

Geez, fuck! No wonder Lori does what she does, Matt thought.

"Hey, Chief. I'm good. How 'bout you?" Matt asked, genuinely curious. The guy looked like he was seconds away from dropping dead of a heart attack.

"Never better," he said with debris and food particles falling down his shirt and onto the table. "So, the old man tells me you're looking for a gig."

"Actually, Vic said you guys could use some help at the station. I thought that maybe my skills and training might come in handy."

"Woah, woah, woah now! I don't think we need *those* kinda skills 'round here. But how 'bout we start you off with some filing and paperwork? And, if you prove yourself, we can go from there."

"Absolutely, Chief. Anything I can do to ease the load."

"Well, that settles it. Now, if you'll excuse me, I have a 10:30 meeting with the mayor. It was great seeing you, Matty boy. We'll catch up again in the next few days. Lacey will help you process all your paperwork. Oh, and sorry to hear about that thing with your old man and your mom." Matt knew this was Leroy's last jab in his power play.

"Yeah, thanks," Matt said matter-of-factly.

"A damn shame, a man beating on his family like that." Leroy muttered as he walked out smelling of ego, fried chicken, and body odor.

Maybe I'll screw his wife, Matt thought to himself, silently seething. *We'll see who's in charge then.*

He went home feeling strange. It was like he was at ease being surrounded by all those guys. It was the closest feeling to home he had since coming back, although that wasn't saying much. He drank his whiskey from the bottle and it eased his raw emotions, but it didn't take long for those feelings to come back. Before he drifted into the numbness of catatonia, he saw his mom's face, blood pouring from a hole in her head.

CHAPTER SIX

Smooth as Honey

M att awoke with a dull ache and throbbing in his temples. The only way he could ease it was by taking a few swigs of vodka directly from the bottle. He showered, got dressed, and made his way to work.

For the next three weeks, each day unfolded in a monotonous sequence, starkly contrasting the rigor of his six months at the police academy. Matt's mornings began with a shot, a ritual that numbed him more than awakened. He showered, got dressed, and headed to work. He did paperwork and not much else, came home, drowned himself in a bottle of Jack, and passed out on the sofa. The mundanity of everyday life led him to desperately seek some sort of outlet, something to break up the monotony. One day, he got more than he bargained for.

After three weeks of doing scut work, Matt was summoned when George, one of the officers who was supposed to be on duty, called in sick with a stomach bug. It wasn't that there were any emergencies or that they were particularly busy, but they were left with only three officers on the streets. Reluctantly, the chief conceded that the inexperienced ex-soldier was his best option.

The day went off without a hitch, with Matt even getting to reprimand a guy who had been shouting obscenities at one of the shopkeepers in town. With his stripes informally earned, he took on the role permanently and reported each day in uniform, ready to head out on patrol.

It was a warm Tuesday. Everywhere was stifling, and the cheap fans were whirring and blowing all around the station. Although it was uncomfortable, Matt thought it was a luxury compared to the sandbox of Iraq, where temperatures could reach highs of over 104°F. Still, everyone around him voiced their complaints.

The day was still and quiet, and Matt and the other officers were engaged in lighthearted conversation. They barely noticed the call coming in and Lacey's quick onset of hysteria as she tried to calm the person on the other end of the line.

"Yes. Oh my God! Sue?! Oh my God! Okay, calm down, I'm gonna dispatch officers right now. I need you to take a deep breath. Everything is going to be fine. The officers will be there before you know it." By this point, Lacey was trying to suppress the panic in her voice.

After a few seconds, she hung up, and turned to the officers. With tears streaming down her face, she said, "There's been a shooting at 148 Whitfield Lane. There's reports of one fatality, to be confirmed when the ambulance arrives."

It took a second for everyone to process what had happened before all the officers were mobilized. Matt was trained for this; he was used to moving with precision and at pace. It wasn't until he was halfway out the door that he realized the address.

"148 Whitfield Lane, Lacey?" he called back. She nodded her head, her expression telling him everything he needed to know. His face dropped as he felt his stomach churn.

"Come on, Groover, we have to go!" Davies called out from the car.

Everything seemed to move in slow motion, even though the speedometer read 80. His breath was racing but the sound in his ears seemed to barely register. He felt like his vision was obscured with blinders, unable to see what was ahead or on either side of him. It seemed to take a lifetime to arrive at the scene. Even though the sirens were blaring, all he heard was a muffled sound, coupled with the pounding of his heartbeat, loud enough to shatter his eardrums.

There, before them, stood the looming figure of a house that, from the outside, looked as simple and as calm as any neighborhood in this part of town. However, it was what was beyond the door that worried him, the people he knew lived there.

Matt sat in the car for, perhaps, just a second longer than he should have, staring at the house he had spent so many of his younger years in. Although it appeared much smaller now that he was fully grown, it appeared to be looming, its intruding and unnecessarily bold figure casting a menacing shadow on him and the other cars in the driveway.

He tried to will himself, to force himself to move. His legs, as heavy as lead, could barely make their way out of the vehicle. The lights of the squad car cast a strange eerie glow on its surroundings, despite it being broad daylight—the red and blue hues adding a cartoonish taint to the unavoidable reality he knew he was about to face.

He thought he had left the gruesome death of war back in the desert, but it seemed to have stretched its fierce grasp all the way to this mundane and quiet suburban town.

Matt put one foot over the threshold and was immediately met with an excruciating, gut-wrenching, ear-splitting scream. It never dulled but rather continued, a wailing, guttural cry that made his stomach flip. The source of the sound was Sue, sitting on the floor, rocking back and forth. Matt made his way toward her, and that was when he noticed the body that lay on the ground between them.

There on the floor, with his legs in an awkward V-shape and his arms wide open, lay his best friend, Chris. He was on the cold hard tiles, spread eagle with a revolver still in his right hand. Matt eyed the two gaping, bleeding holes that had taken up permanent residence in Chris's head, piercing his temples.

The frustration began welling up in Matt's mind as he knew he was taking a second too long to process and understand what was going on. When he was on active duty, he struggled to get his body to keep up with his mind; he was always ahead of the kill. But now, his brain was lagging like an antique computer.

Then, something clicked and it all began to make sense. Chris had been honorably discharged from duty when his entire unit successfully captured an Al-Qaeda military leader, but not before most of his platoon was slaughtered right before his eyes. They all laid down their lives so he could successfully capture the target, leaving him to return home in a plane full of boxes.

Matt took in the scene and couldn't help but draw a contrast between this and his life in the military. Blood didn't belong in a home that was clean, well-kept, had white tiles, and a wall full of family photos. He looked at Chris' head. The entire right hand side had been burned and brutalized, unrecognizable by the mere force and impact of the bullet that had been discharged from point blank range. The blood oozed in a pool around the body. *That's all he was now, a body, a lifeless mannequin, cold and still.*

The blood had started to coagulate around the wound. The splatters on the wall to the left of him covered photos of a smiling wedding day, of a pregnancy, of a baby's face—a child who was now going to come home from school and hear that their daddy was a victim of the war, a battle that was lost in his own living room.

"For God sake," he heard his partner cry to one of the attending officers. "Get her out of here, won't you? She shouldn't have to see her husband lying there like that."

Matt had seen a lot in the sandbox. He had seen limbs torn from torsos, intestines dangling from friends who still somehow managed to have a bit of life in them, but something about the contrast of his friend's dark red blood dripping from a photo of his only child made him sick to his stomach.

He fought the urge to vomit, the need to get out of there and breathe some fresh air. He still couldn't process that Chris was gone, that the guy he had spent long summers with—carving their names on park benches, talking to girls, smoking cheap cigarettes—was no longer drawing breath.

"Shit, Chris," he said. "You could have at least talked to me, man. You could have picked up the phone."

A young EMT—Joshua Harding, his name badge said—approached the body, stooping down to examine it. He saw Matt standing there, whispered a word to the forensics team, and they hastily moved away.

"I'm so sorry. Chris was a great guy," Joshua said, placing a hand on his shoulder. "I can give you a moment, if you want."

"It's okay," Matt replied, gritting his teeth. "The job's gotta be done."

He stood there looking at his pal and, for some reason, he struggled to summon a memory of their time together. Everything seemed so distant, too far off to grab on to. He couldn't think of a moment when they laughed or cried together.

But then, just as he was about to walk away, a memory landed like a feather gently descending on an undisturbed pond. He thought about a conversation that he and Chris had as teenagers.

"Hey Matt, you're almost a man. Grown up, almost done with school. Life is gonna begin soon, man," Chris *said, his voice carrying the laughter that always seemed to be seconds away.*

"Yeah, boy? Well, you only got about two years on me, and I've been a grown up my whole life. Had to, what with my daddy the way he is."

"You're a jackass is what you are," Chris laughed.

Matt couldn't help but smile as they looked out over the lake, sipping soda as if they were getting their beer buzz on.

"But fo' real, man, whatcha gonna do after graduation?"

"I dunno, haven't given it much thought." They sat in silence for a while before Matt spoke again. "Actually, I have been thinkin' about somethin'. I was thinking I

might enlist in the army. You know, help sort out that shit that's going down in Iraq."

"Ha, you? You'll probably only end up pushing paperwork with arms as weak as those." He slapped Matt's biceps, but they both knew that Matt was telling the truth. He just had to get away from everything that was going on at home. *"Well, I guess you can't go out there alone. I reckon, maybe I'll join you."*

"Nah, boy. You got Sue. I know you'll marry her the second you get a chance," Matt chuckled.

"Yeah, and if all goes to plan, I'll be deployed after my honeymoon."

"You're being serious?" Matt asked.

"As serious as you are. Where you go, I follow. Like always," he held out his fist and Matt bumped it with his own.

They'd never spoken about that conversation after that day, but before Matt had even enlisted, Chris had headed out. The first Matt knew of it was when he got a letter from overseas, and Chris recounted how he'd gotten into a fist fight on his first day at the base with some *"fancy boy from Florida"* who tried to tell Chris which bunk he should be sleeping on.

Matt thought about that memory, the guilt of his loss. He stood there, questioning if he did this to Chris, if he had inadvertently convinced him to enlist. He was interrupted by Davies walking out of the kitchen, Sue's soft sobs emanating through the gap between the door and the jamb.

Davies stood next to him and looked down at the body, whispering a silent prayer and making the gesture of the cross. "You should probably head in there," he told Matt. "She's asking for you."

Matt walked into the kitchen, leaving the EMT and forensics to get on with their work. Sue sat at the table, visibly shaking and quivering, her eyes red-rimmed with the scars of so many tears. She looked beaten, destroyed.

"He–hey," Matt said, standing beside her. The words struggled to escape and got caught in his dry throat. *What do you even say to the wife of your dead best friend? A man who just, literally, blew his brains out all over their family photos?*

"Oh, Matty," she crumbled into heaving sobs, pushing her face against his chest. He stood there, trying to fight back every ounce of tears, gripping her as if at any moment she might slip away from him.

It took a few minutes, but she finally calmed down.

"Wh—what happened? He seemed fine when I saw him at Marshall's."

"Oh, he was. He was doin' real good. But, in the past few weeks, he started gettin' stuck in his own mind. He was withdrawn. He even started sleeping on the couch because of the night terrors he was having. But today," she looked off into the distance, "today, he was worse somehow." Matt listened, knowing that the internal scars of war not only hurt the people on the front line, but they affected loved ones, family members, and friends. It was the toxic cycle of war. No one was immune. "He went to the store. I told him what he needed to get, but he forgot the eggs. It wasn't a big deal. I told him it wasn't a big deal," she caught a sob in the back of her throat. "I didn't even know he had his gun on him. He kept arguing and saying that I never told him to get eggs. He kept at it until he gave up fighting. His last words were "fuck it," and then he pulled the trigger."

She broke down again, burying herself in Matt's arms, her shoulders shuddering and heaving.

"I–I don't know what to say, Sue. I am so, so sorry."

"I need you to promise me something, Matt," she turned to him and held his hands in her own. "Get help! Please! The war did this, and I know it's eating away at you, too. Don't let it do to you what it did to him. Please. Promise me. *Please!*"

He got in the car and headed back to the station with Davies. On the way, he called Marshall to let him know. He knew they would start preparations immediately, but he couldn't stay there a second longer—not with Chris's blood scattered in places it should have never been.

As soon as he got back to base, the chief approached him, his face a mask of solemnity. He immediately sent him home. "Take all the time you need," he said, patting his shoulder. "He was a good man, your pal. A good one, alright."

Matt left the station but he knew that going home was not an option. Instead, he made his way to the bar. He was going to face this loss the only way he knew how.

Hours passed, and he had long stopped feeling, both emotionally and physically. Although his senses were dulled, he felt a figure move behind him, the body moving with the music. She spoke and her voice was as smooth as honey, a southern drawl he didn't recognize but that melted his insides as every word dripped off her tongue. He smelled her perfume, sweetly delicious, entirely blowing his mind away.

"I'll have whatever he's having."

CHAPTER SEVEN
54 Calls

Matt looked up at her, his head swimming and his mind fuzzy. If he wasn't drunk before, the sight of the exceptionally attractive young woman sitting next to him certainly sent his brain into a tailspin.

"So, what does it take 'round here to push someone to day drink?" she asked, smiling. Her bright blue eyes twinkled in the dimly lit bar.

"Ha, honey, you don't wanna know."

"Try me," she replied, her lips curled ever so slightly.

"Well," his words sounded slurred. "My best friend just blew his brains out in front of his wife because he had PTSD from the war, you know? But that's not even the best part." He was laughing now. "The best part is that it could have been me. I was in the war too. Sometimes, I wanna do the same damn thing." He knocked back the rest of his drink.

Her expression darkened. "That seems like a good enough reason to me." She smiled awkwardly and stood up to walk away.

"Hey, hey, wait. I'm sorry. It's been a rough day. I swear, I'm not usually an asshole. Right, Rick?" Matt asked the bartender.

"He's usually an asshole," Rick laughed.

The woman paused before offering her hand. "I'm Tiffany. Nice to meet ya."

"Hi, Tiffany, I'm Matt. The pleasure is all mine." He shook it and took her in. She was a bombshell alright, small in stature with long blond waves that reached down to her waist. She had bright blue eyes that contrasted against her sun-kissed skin. She wore a cherry colored gloss on her lips that accentuated her smile in a way that really caught him off guard.

They spent the afternoon at the bar and she told him that she was visiting family. They drank and ate, and it wasn't long before they were walking back to his apartment.

"Look, I don't usually go home with men I just met."

"I never took you for the type that did," he said, smiling. It was warm and the breeze of the evening danced across his skin, which was already tingling with an alcohol buzz. He took it in and breathed deeply as Tiffany's perfume carried on the wind.

She laughed. "Well, it seemed like you've been to hell and back. Kinda looked like you could use someone, and I've been told that I have a knack for taking in sad cases."

"Oh, I'm a sad case now, am I?" he teased.

"You, sir, are the saddest of 'em all," she laughed and walked ahead. He pulled her arm and twirled her toward him and looked into her eyes. He didn't know if it was the alcohol or the fact that she was the most exquisite and satiating woman he had ever laid eyes on, but his mind went around in circles as he looked at her.

Slowly, he leaned in and their lips made contact. It had been weeks since he had felt a woman's skin against his own. In stark contrast with the hard realities of war, a woman's body was a soft place to land.

He didn't know how they got to his apartment, or even how they unlocked the door. Just, for a brief second, he felt ashamed at the state of his place, but luckily, she only had eyes for him. Again, they kissed. He felt her breathing hitch and quicken as she put her hands around him, her body pressed against his. His hands dropped down to her hips and then down to her thighs. Her skin was smooth as silk beneath her denim shorts.

Within seconds, they were undressed and their bodies were intertwined on his sofa, writhing in pure ecstasy and unbridled desire, the likes of which Matt had long forgotten. In comparison to the rest of his life, this was as beautifully simple as it was going to get.

He awoke the next morning, and within seconds, he was hit with the awkwardness that had now become routine after his nights of heavy drinking. His mouth was dry, his eyes strained against the light streaming in from the window. His body seemed to be floating, moving slower than he willed it.

It took him a while to regain his bearings. It wasn't until a few seconds later, when the recollection of the day before came flooding back, that he realized those few waking moments were a relief from everything else that had almost battered him into submission.

He was reminded of the death of his colleague, Kenzo, the murder of the woman he called his mother, the loss of his best friend. Inch by inch, everything came back, and then he remembered Tiffany, the blonde bombshell who had helped to quell the pain.

He wished he could remember the satisfaction from the night before in detail, but he couldn't break through the alcohol shield that blocked out much of it.

As he composed himself and found his space in the house, he realized that Tiffany was nowhere to be found. He sat up and felt a sharp pang through the front of his head. He rubbed his eyes and tried to ease the pain. Just then, he heard someone approach from the kitchen.

"You literally have nothin' to eat or drink around here," Tiffany said, walking into the room with a glass of water. "You actually don't have much of anything at all." She handed the glass to him.

She was wearing his white t-shirt from the day before, the one he wore under his uniform. Her legs seemed to go on for days, and the shirt stopped just short of her bottom. He certainly enjoyed the vantage point he had, sitting beneath her on the bed.

"Yeah, I can't even offer to make yourself at home," he said, taking the glass and gulping the cold liquid.

He looked at the time and realized that he was meant to be at the station 20 minutes ago.

"Oh, shit, I'm late for work. Uh, listen, I'm not running out on you. You really can make yourself at home if you like, but I'm late for work. I'll be back later this evening, alright?" he made his way to the bathroom, but stopped in the doorway before leaving. "I should probably get your number, shouldn't I?" he smiled awkwardly.

"You probably should."

Tiffany shot him that seductive smile and crippled him all over again.

When he walked into the station, everyone awkwardly maneuvered around him, walking gingerly as if on eggshells. It didn't help that he looked like hell. He went to his desk, trying to avoid the sorrowful glares and anxious nods, but it wasn't long before Davies came to him and suggested he go home.

"It's a rough time, man. We know you two were tight. Why don't you go home? Go help your family make preparations, maybe help Sue. Come back when you've had time to process it. No one expects you to be here, man."

"If I go home, all I am going to think about is what happened. I need to keep busy," he said.

"Yeah, I get it, trust me. But the chief won't let you stick around if ya head ain't clear. I say, take the time, head home, and relax a bit. We'll see you on Monday."

Matt packed himself up and headed toward the door. He found himself hoping that Tiffany would still be at his apartment, waiting for him. On the drive home, his mind wandered, thinking of everything that had gone down. *Was he the human version of poison? Was he bad news?* It seemed that everyone close to him was either dead or hurting.

When he got home, he found the apartment was empty. Tiffany was gone, and if it wasn't for the lingering smell of her perfume, he might have doubted that the night before had happened at all. He made his way into the kitchen and grabbed the vodka bottle. It was his only companion now.

He took a swig and sat down to watch some TV. Before he could bring the bottle to his mouth a second time, his phone rang. It was Marshall.

"Funeral preparations have been made," his brother said. "Three weeks on Thursday, at the Church of the Holy Saint."

"That was quick," Matt replied. "His body's barely even cold."

"It's for the best. Sue wants it this way."

Matt set down the phone and took another hit. He didn't know how he was going to get through everything, at least not without dulling his emotions. Marshall had been helping Sue with everything, and the truth was, Matt didn't want to help. He needed to keep as far away from that painful task as possible. All he wanted to do was bury himself deep in Tiffany and drown out reality with hard liquor.

He called her.

"I wanted to see if you fancied some dinner tonight?" he asked, trying to inject some joy into his tone.

"Do I have any options or are you gonna serve me some pickle juice and whiskey for dinner?" she asked.

"Well, you could either have me for dinner. Or we could have some Chinese."

She laughed slightly and he enjoyed the sound. "Sure, what time should I come over?"

"Yeah, well, they sent me home from work. So... anytime really."

It didn't take more than 20 minutes for her to get there, and they did anything but eat.

The days leading up to Chris's funeral went by in a blur of sex and booze. Like photos tainted by age, a few moments stood out in snippets for him. He remembered the passion and frantic fucking. He remembered drinking enough to forget, and somehow, without remembering anything else, he remembered standing beside a grave. Everything seemed to occur through tunnel vision, a narrow lens that only allowed the bare minimum to shine through.

What he did remember, however, was the flag. It was always the flag, folded neatly and handed to the mourning widow, as if it could take the place of a husband and father. As if it could erase the sickness that had wormed its way into Chris's brain.

Over the weeks that came, he was plagued by fear, anxiety, and the crippling and recurring dreams of war. The only difference is that in dreams, among the scattered remains of those who he fought beside, was Chris, laying splayed out on the sand with a gunshot wound in his head.

Matt also found himself increasingly more aware of himself. When he woke up from his dreams, he would be covered in sweat and would find himself wondering when it would be his turn. The stress and anxiety seemed like it was too much to bear. He was barely holding things together.

One day, a few weeks after Chris's death, he rocked up at the station and was called into the chief's office.

"Look, Matt, I know it's been a couple of weeks since your friend passed, and I just want to let you know that it's fine if you take some more time off for yourself. You need to mentally and emotionally come to terms with the reality you've faced. We also have counseling services available, not just for civilians, but for our guys too. You're encouraged to use this service. I know, after Chris, a lot of the guys went for counseling, and I thought—"

"Sorry, Chief, but I'm good. I don't need time. It's happened. We move on."

"Matt, I'm gonna be frank with you. There have been some, well, concerns about you. Now, I need you to know, this is just because people care."

"Have I done something wrong?" Matt felt an anger rising within him, and he fought to get it under control. *What I wouldn't do for a drink right now*, he thought.

"No, no, we know and understand what you have been going through. But some of the guys have noticed that you've been coming in consistently late, that you're reeking of alcohol, and that, sometimes, you seem a little drunk. Now, I know that alcohol can serve as a great tool to numb the pain, but in your role, you are dealing with life and death situations. It cannot be tainted or obscured by liquor." Matt put his head down, not knowing how to respond. He knew he couldn't deny it. "I'm not gonna take any disciplinary action against you because I understand your circumstances. Instead, I'm gonna give you some time off to pull yourself together. Take a couple of weeks to figure yourself out, but most importantly, take the time to heal. You've been a great addition to the force and we don't want to lose you. Work on yourself. Come back stronger."

Matt sat there in silence, his head bowed as an endless stream of thoughts went through his mind. *I should insult this fat pig for trying to take my job away from me. I should tell him how I fucked his wife—how everyone on this side of town did. I should tell him what an embarrassment he is to the police force. But what is that gonna get me? We gotta respect our superiors. And he ain't wrong. FUCK! What is wrong with me? How did I get so broken? What do I do now?*

He sat there in silence, unmoving. The chief shifted awkwardly in his chair, and the atmosphere thickened like syrup. Finally, he looked up and shook his head. *What the hell?*

Without a word, he stood up, and put his hand out to shake his boss'. Then, he turned and walked out of the office, out of the station, and straight to the bar. He never worked another day on the force again.

Yet another blurry day went by. Another day of everything moving by with him not having any control. Another day of alcohol leading the way and of him aimlessly following.

Matt didn't know how, but he ended up at home, surrounded by half-consumed bottles of whiskey. He thought of his dad, of the man he had been. "I'm becoming you, man," he said. "You win. I can't fight it. I'm no better than you. I'm no fucking better."

His body ached, his muscles hurt, and everything felt like a strain. The only comfort he took was that when he passed out in a drunken stupor, but only because it kept the dreams at bay.

He stood and tried to get to the bathroom. It was there, in the mirror, where he saw bruises all over his body. The remnants of a night long forgotten, the pain sending lightning across his head. He didn't know what happened, if he got in a fight, fell down some stairs, or got hit by a car.

After he washed his face and tried to place the events of the night before, he began looking for his phone. He was shocked to see 54 missed calls, 50 of which were from Tiffany. He called her back.

"Where the fuck are you? I've been trying to get a hold of you since yesterday afternoon," she yelled over the phone without even saying hello. The panic in her voice was real, and while he was touched by her concern, he was annoyed that he now had someone to answer to.

"Hey, I'm fine, I swear. I had a hectic day."

"Yeah, I heard all about your hectic day," she spat the words at him, her mouth dripping with disgust. "Where are you now?"

"I'm at home, but I don't want you comin' over here if you're just gonna yell at me." He knew it was an abysmal attempt to ease the tension with humor. It didn't work.

"We need to talk. I'm on my way to you now." She hung up and he glared at the door. *What the hell was he going to do now?*

CHAPTER EIGHT

Free Pass

He threw water over his face, freshened up, and brushed his teeth, hoping that the scent of mint would mask the booze on his breath. Then, he headed for the living room, where the floor was barely visible under empty bottles and discarded pizza boxes.

Matt quickly grabbed a black, plastic sack and threw everything inside, tying a knot and tossing it outside in the trash bin. The apartment still smelled of whiskey and sweat, so he grabbed his can of body spray and delivered a few puffs in each room. He wrinkled his nose, realizing that the mixture of the sweet smelling Axe with the dense, pungent stink of his apartment was actually worse than it had been before.

Before he could do anything to rectify the situation, there was a knock at the door.

"Hi," he said, moving aside to let Tiffany enter. She looked and smelled great, but her face said something else entirely. "You okay?"

"No, I'm fucking not okay," she hissed, whirling on him. "Where the hell have you been?"

"I've been right here."

"No you haven't," she replied. "I called. No answer. I went to the bar. They hadn't seen you. I even called your brother."

Matt slumped onto the couch and waited for the room to stop spinning. He didn't know what was worse, knowing he was in a bad place or not remembering anything at all since Chris's funeral. Everything was just a smeared picture of colors and sounds, none of which made sense to him.

"I'm sorry," he said. "I am. I don't know what's happening to me."

Tiffany took the chair opposite. "You're fucked up, Matt. That's what's happening. You've got a lot going on in your head, a lot of shit swirling around in there, and I don't know how to help you. I don't even know if I've got the energy to try."

He ran a hand across his face, and tried to wipe the fog away. Everything seemed like it was moving in slow motion, as if they were swimming in molasses. His head hurt and his mouth was as dry as concrete. His muscles ached, too, as if he'd been in a boxing match with a world champ.

"I can't expect you to try if I can't even help myself," he said. She shrugged as she picked a piece of cotton from her dress and dabbed at her lipstick. "Can I make you something?" he asked, suddenly energized. He got to his feet and half stumbled. "Dinner? A drink?"

She shook her head. "No, I'm fine."

He eyed her up and down. She looked good, too good. *What had she even seen in him? Sure, he kept himself in shape and didn't look half bad when he made the effort, but she was Hollywood style attractive, sunset strip class gorgeous.* He felt a stirring in his groin. "You wanna—you know?"

"Jesus, Matt!" She stood and went to the window.

"Well, I don't know, do I?" he yelled, glaring at the last remnants of whiskey in the one bottle he hadn't fully consumed. "I'm not a mind reader."

"No, you're not." She followed his gaze. "You're thinking of pouring yourself another glass, aren't you?"

He wiped the back of his hand across his mouth and shook his head. He had to admit, the thought had crossed his mind. In fact, it was pulling at him as if he were on a long rope, being dragged toward it like bank robbers being pulled behind a bounty hunter's wagon.

"No," he said. "I'm not thirsty."

"Didn't you say your old man was an alcoholic? That's why he killed your mom."

"What?"

"Your mom? The woman your father smashed over the head with a hammer."

"You don't get to talk about her," he hissed.

Tiffany seemed to sense she'd hit her mark, turning and walking toward him, her high heels clicking against the hard tile, her hips swinging with every step. "Hit her in the head with a hammer because she wouldn't let him go to the bar to get his next high."

"I'm warning you, Tiffany. I'm not in the mood for this."

She wasn't about to stop. He could see the fire had ignited behind her piercing blue eyes, her lips curling at the corners, her long red nails protruding like those of a big cat. "A chip off the old block, wouldn't you say? The apple doesn't fall far from the tree." She leaned toward him, her eyes wide. "Does it?"

Just then, the gasket blew in his head, and he shot her a look he only ever reserved for his enemies. He went for her, screaming obscenities, followed by poisonous, hateful things.

"You're just a two bit hooker, you know that, right? I only got in the sack with you because you made it so easy. I didn't even have to try. One look from me and you were on your back, legs spread like a cheap Vegas whore! You're a slut, a cheap piece of meat. You're not even worth my time!"

"You bastard!"

"Go back to the hole you crawled out of! I don't need you here. I don't need your negativity, your constant whining, or your endless bitching and moaning. The sex wasn't even good. While I was screwing you, I was thinking about being with someone else. It didn't matter who, just as long as it wasn't you, you fucking bitch!"

The look on her face was one of shock and indignation. She burst into tears, glaring at him as if he had struck her. He didn't move, didn't flinch. He was numb. He couldn't believe what had just happened. All of a sudden, he was snapped back into the world of the conscious, as if the alcohol had instantly evaporated from his body.

"Oh shit," he said. "Tiffany, I'm sorry." He moved toward her, trying to comfort her, but she pulled away, her body side on to him with her hands held out, flapping in the air.

"Get away from me," she said. "Get your hands away from me, you bastard."

"I didn't mean to, I—" he couldn't find the right words. "I don't know why I said those things."

She turned to him and he could see the tears in her eyes, but more than that, her expression was that of a terrified child. *What had he done to her?*

"I don't let any man talk to me that way," she said, grabbing her things. "This is over."

"Tiffany, no! That's not me, I'm not that person. I swear!" He glanced at the whiskey bottle once more and thought of Chris lying there in the casket, his head glued back together. He thought of his mother, or at least the woman who had raised him. He thought of Kenzo bleeding out on the sand like a cheap piece of meat. Above all, he thought of the man who had struck him with his belt buckle more times than he cared to remember. "You goaded me," he said, turning away. "You were pressing my buttons."

He heard Tiffany laugh, but it was a nervous one.

"Shit, you think that's okay, do you? Just because I mentioned what your father did, you think that gives you the right to call me those names, those awful things? To scare me like that?"

"I didn't say that," he stumbled over his words, unable to properly form his thoughts. "But you did. You knew how to hurt me, and you used it against me."

Tiffany grabbed her stuff from the bedside table, picked up the shoes she'd left behind during her last visit, and scoffed. "You want to change your luck,

Matt? It starts with you. You can't keep blaming everybody else for what's happened. Sure, you had a shit time as a kid. Sure, you had to endure hell out there in the sandbox. Yeah, you've had tragedy after tragedy since you came back," she pointed at him. "But that, in no way, excuses what you just did or how you've been treating everyone around you these past few weeks. You don't get a free pass just because you're an ex-soldier. You have to earn respect. You have to earn love. You can't just act like a bastard and assume everyone around you will give you the time and space to heal. Life doesn't work like that."

She placed her hand on the door as her shoulders started to shudder. The tears came once more, long and slow, dripping from the point of her chin as she fought to compose herself.

He watched her from a distance, thinking about how they'd met, how she'd given him a few moments of joy, and how she'd made him forget and push everything away. Sure, she was a funtime gal and they'd only gotten together for a few laughs, a bit of shared carnal pleasure, but somehow he'd even made a mess of a casual relationship. He needed a drink and he needed one soon. A hangover was looming like a dark cloud, threatening to drag him down into its primordial soup.

"Are you going?" he asked. "You don't want to stay a while? I'll make it up to you, I swear. Whatever you want, it's on me. Anything."

"You really don't get it, do you? There's no making up for this. There's nothing you can do to make this right. I'm going, Matt, and I'm not coming back."

He tried to think of the words that could somehow make her change her mind, but everything drew him back to the image of a swirling liquid in a glass with a couple of cubes of ice thrown in for good measure. He couldn't push past that, no matter how hard he tried.

"Then, why did you even come over?"

Her head fell against the door as she closed her eyes. "I came to tell you that I'm pregnant."

CHAPTER NINE

Isaiah 55:7

They say a casket only needs a few nails to seal it tight—hell, three or four would probably do the trick, just fine—but the one that was delivered into the box that Matt found himself in on that fateful night was about as decisive as they came. Not only had he terrified a woman, something that made him feel sick to his stomach, but this particular woman was also carrying his child.

He went into a tailspin, wondering how the hell he'd dug himself such a deep hole. It felt like he was clawing at damp earth, drenched in rainwater, the worms snaking through his hair and slithering under his clothes. He couldn't breathe, couldn't think. All he could see was his dad's face in his prison cell, grinning at him maniacally, a bloody hammer in one hand and a glass of bourbon in the other.

"I'm not you," he hissed, spitting and hateful. "I am not you!"

He tried to call Tiffany but her phone just rang, and she wouldn't answer his texts. He even tried going to her place and banging on the door, but her shades were drawn and the lights were off. If she was home, she was doing a good job of hiding from him, and why shouldn't she? He had scared her and he had hurt her, maybe not physically, but the outcome was the same.

He stood on the street, waiting for the door to the bar to open, the rain cascading down his face. *What was he becoming? Who was he?* No job, no family to speak of, no friends. The people who stood by him were the ones he had killed for, the ones he had fought beside, but every time he thought of that hellhole in the desert, lightning flashes fizzed across his temples and he wanted to curl up in a ball.

His options were limited, but one singular thought kept playing over and over in his mind on repeat. *Finish it. End it. Do everyone a favor and check out.*

He kept thinking of Chris. *Chris with the gun in his hand, the hole in his temple, his brains splattered across the picture frames, his wife sobbing uncontrollably on the sofa.* Chris had left behind a family that loved him, a family that wanted him in their lives. The emotional destruction that lay in his wake was immense, almost too heart wrenching to bear. But the difference between Chris and Matt was that Chris had people, he had something to live for, even if he didn't see it. What did Matt have? A brother who wasn't blood and a father who was serving thirty to life.

When Rick opened the door, he hurried inside, shaking the drips from his hair and coat.

"Little early, aren't ya?" Rick asked.

"The usual," Matt replied, impatiently tapping the counter. "And stack 'em up. I'm in for the duration."

He had very little memory of what happened next. One minute, he was knocking back a double Jamieson's, the next he was by the jukebox, trying to get the thing to play a "damn Skynyrd song." Later, there were three guys standing beside him, laughing, making all sorts of noise.

Matt remembered accusing them of mocking him, suggesting the guy in the middle should go "screw his momma." The next thing he knew, he was outside swinging wildly, taking one in the jaw before another guy slammed a knee into his ribs. He blacked out, and when he came round, Rick's face filled his vision, telling him to "go home, get outta here."

Everything went black once more, and he awoke on his floor, vomit on the carpet and in his mouth.

"I've had enough," he said. "This is enough."

He went to his bedroom, crashing into the table, knocking chairs onto the ground, and tripping over empty bottles. The bedside drawer lay open, his underwear spilling from its wide mouth. He rummaged through its contents, looking for the one thing he needed more than anything. The one thing that could make the pain stop. It wasn't there, the damn thing wasn't there. A book fell to the ground, smashing into his bare foot. He yelled out and stepped away.

It was in the rear pocket of his jeans, the gun. He must have grabbed it before he passed out. It was loaded too, a clip full of bullets.

"There you are," he said. "There the hell you are."

He held the weapon in his hands, cool and smooth like ice. It was comforting to him, but terrifying, too. He hadn't fired a gun since Iraq, nor had he wanted to. The deafening crack made his body convulse. Guns had been his salvation and his curse, but perhaps this one was different. Perhaps this one would be his cure. This one would make the nightmares end, the anger dissipate. He glared at it as if it were an enemy and a lover all in the same breath.

"What d'ya say, fella?" he asked. "We gonna do this or what?"

He pulled his reading chair beside his bed and sat down, suddenly feeling like he could collapse at any moment. He caught his reflection in the mirror. Dark eyes, hair that needed cutting, a beard that hadn't been trimmed for forever. His shirt was stained with vomit, his mouth bloodied, and his pants covered in grime from the street. He looked like a hobo, as if he'd spent the last month on the streets.

"Jesus, man. How did you let it come to this?"

He held the gun tight, like the rope from a rescue boat. He turned it toward him and peered down the barrel. He knew there was a lead projectile in there, traveling at 1,200 feet per second, that would turn his brain to mush and his skull into so many shattered fragments. All he had to do was pull the trigger. *Just one little, innocuous act. One moment in time, one frame in a three hour movie.*

He closed his eyes, placed the barrel in his mouth. The carbon steel was cold and hard against his tongue and teeth. Everything flashed before him: His discussion with Chris by the lake, signing up for the military, the journey overseas, the heat of the desert, the first shots fired, bullets striking his platoon, the blood, the screams, the roar of detonating explosives, his father raining down hammer blows on his mom, Kenzo lying in a casket, Chris's motionless body lying in a pool of his own piss. And then there was Tiffany. Tiffany and the child he would never know. The child who would never know his father.

He opened his eyes and saw it. The book that had landed on his foot. It was open at Isaiah 55:7, a verse he knew well from church. He said it out loud, recoiling at the sound of his own voice. He was crying.

"Let the wicked forsake their ways," he began, lowering the gun, "and the unrighteous their thoughts. Let them turn to the Lord, and he will have mercy on them, and to our God, for he will freely pardon."

The gun fell from his lap as he leaned forward, holding the book in his hands, feeling the warmth of the paper, smelling the ink and the musty jacket.

Maybe there was another way. *Just maybe.*

The one thing his father had made them do when they were kids, one thing that Matt had come to enjoy above all else, was attend church every Sunday. They never missed it, not even when they had birthdays or were sick. His father would tell him, "the church looks after everybody, no matter what they've done or who they are. And, because of that, our lord and savior Jesus Christ deserves our dedication and constant, unrelenting presence."

Matt hadn't cared. It was the one moment in his week where he didn't feel like he was about an inch from getting accused of something he hadn't done or struck across the spine with the buckle of his father's belt. The church was a place of peace, where they listened to stories from exotic lands, sung songs at the top of their lungs, and chatted to people they barely even knew.

Matt hadn't attended since he'd signed up for the Army. He'd forgotten his faith. War does that to you. When the devil was waiting outside your door every goddamn day, your only god was the gun in your hands and the knife in your belt. Hymns seemed impotent on the battlefield, with prayer being just a collection of jumbled words that meant nothing.

Sitting there in his apartment, reacquainting himself with the good book while drinking strong black coffee, Matt began to believe that everything that had happened to him was because of that one simple truth: He had forgotten God. He had let God down.

He had strayed from the flock, maybe a little too far for the shepherd to bring him home.

Well, he was here now. *He was back.*

He headed down to the Church of the Holy Saint. The last time he was there, they were burying Chris, and Matt had barely been in the land of the living. Now, he was wide awake, maybe for the first time since he had returned home, and he could see clearly. He could see his sins, where he had strayed from the path.

"You looking for something, son?" a man asked. He was dressed in a Stevie Ray Vaughan T-Shirt, blue jeans, and leather boots. "You look like a man who has something on his mind and needs someone to unload it on."

Matt stood on the sidewalk, looking up at the building's tall spire. "Maybe I do. Maybe that's exactly what I want."

The man crossed his arms and grinned. "This place holds a lot of memories for me. Some good, some bad. Mostly good though. Met a lot of people, heard a lot of stories, and dried a lot of tears."

"I got a lot of stories of my own."

"We all do, friend. We all do." The door to the church stood half open, and Matt caught a glimpse of the open space beyond, warm, welcoming, and dimly lit by candlelight. "You going in?"

"Thinking about it," Matt replied, not sure if he really believed it.

"He'll be glad to see you, I'm sure."

Matt turned to him. "Who?"

"The big man. JC. The holy spirit. However you refer to him."

"Not sure I'm good company, right now."

"Talk, sit, or take a nap. He won't judge you. You're his child, after all."

The guy seemed to have a lot of answers, and he was persistent as hell.

"Sorry," Matt said. "Who did you say you were again?"

The man held out a hand, a thick palm with cigar-shaped fingers. "Name's McGeever," he said, shooting him a smile as bright as the sun. "But, you can call me Reverend."

CHAPTER TEN

Love Thy Neighbor

Everything after that moment was the same, but different, in so many ways. A few months passed, but Matt was still Matt. His shit show of a life was still a shit show. He got an administration job with the Department of Energy, which was about as dull as they came. He still wanted a drink every second of every minute of every day, and he still dreamed of being back in the sandbox, blood running like wine through the broken streets. He still had an unborn child, slowly growing within the womb of a woman who he had said those terrible things to, and who now couldn't even bear to communicate with him.

However, now he had a place he could go. A place where the pressure could be released, where he could speak openly and without judgment—a place where he could converse with God.

He'd taken to helping out around the place: cleaning, doing some repair work, maintaining the grounds. It kept his dark thoughts at bay and it felt good in his soul, like he was doing the Lord's work, however menial. He found himself looking forward to the Sunday service once more, sitting in the aisles, singing with the congregation, saying prayers, and listening to what the reverend had to say. It was like a community, a family, and he yearned for that. Matt yearned for the connection.

That evening, after the service, he decided he had to try. He had to do everything he could to make it right.

Standing at Tiffany's door, listening to the sound of music playing on the stereo system inside, he felt hopeful. Maybe the Lord would look down kindly on him. If he couldn't be with her anymore, at least they could be civil. He hoped that he could, in some way, make amends for what he had done. He was ready to repent, ready to do whatever it took.

When she opened the door and glared at him, he realized there was no going back.

"My father says if he sees you 'round here, you're gonna find out how handy he is with a hunting knife."

Matt held up his hands. "I'm not here to fight."

"Then why are you here?"

"I've changed, Tiffany. I'm not the man you once knew."

"You were never much of a man before." She ushered him in. "If you're coming inside, make it quick. I got things to do."

He walked into the apartment and was confronted by piles of open suitcases, one of which was filled with baby clothes and diapers.

"Going somewhere?" She didn't answer him. She just folded her arms and looked him up and down. "Listen," he said. "I'm not drinking. I joined AA. I've been sober for three weeks now."

"Give this man a gold star."

"Yeah, I know it's not much, but it's a start."

She cocked her head. "You working again?"

"A little. The Department of Energy, and I'm doing some stuff for the Church of the Holy Saint. Maintenance work mainly."

She laughed. "You found God or something?"

He smiled. "Still looking." They stood that way for a moment, listening to the radio as it played an old Patsy Cline number. "You didn't answer my question," he said, breaking the ice that had formed between them.

"I know," she replied. "Look, say what you gotta say and then go. I told you before, I don't waste my time with men who treat women that way."

He shook his head. "I'm not that man. That isn't me."

"Sure as hell looked like you that night."

"As I said, I've changed."

She turned away. "That's what they all say, but then they go back to the way they always were."

"I won't."

"You did!"

He picked at a finger, looked down at the suitcase with the tiny clothes, the little socks and shoes that were so small you could barely get your thumb in them. He noticed something scary. *They were blue.*

"It's a boy?"

"Gonna be," she replied, holding a hand to her bump. "Still got a ways to go yet."

"We're having a boy?"

"No," she said, waving her hand. "You're not having anything to do with him. This baby's mine and mine alone."

"It takes two to tango, you know."

"And only one to fuck it all up."

He was losing the battle, and he knew it. "I have rights."

"Really? You're claiming that now, are you?" She threw her hand in the air. "You lost any rights you had the minute you behaved the way you did, Matt. And you lost my respect, too."

"I could get a lawyer."

She seemed to think about that for a second. "Look, I wasn't going to tell you this, but I went to my father that night. He wants to kill you, by the way, but instead I convinced him to let me deal with it. He's not a man to be messed with, Matt. He knows people, bad people."

His anger was escalating now. "You threatening me, Tiffany? Because I gotta tell ya, that shit don't work with me."

"If you don't care about yourself," she screamed, "then at least care about your child, your boy. We've got a new life waiting for us, Matt. A guy I've been seeing, he has money, he has a nice place, and he has his own business. He can't have kids of his own, but he wants me and he wants my child." She was crying now. "Don't you see? You can make this alright with just one simple gesture."

He shook his head, barely able to make sense of what she was telling him. All he knew was she was taking his child away, the one thing that could give him focus and the ability to breathe again.

"I don't understand," he said. "What do you want from me?"

She went to him, kissed his cheek, her lips soft and tender. "You have to let us go."

With Tiffany gone for good this time, Matt threw himself into his work. The church couldn't afford to pay him, but he didn't care. He did it for free, occupying his mind with carpentry, repairing cracks in the path, chopping back the undergrowth, and replacing door hinges.

The days in the office were long and the nights in the church were cold, but he barely felt it. When his fingers hurt and his back screamed at him for mercy, he focused on the pain, channeling it into something productive. It helped to push away the desperate desire for liquor.

One day, while he was painting the picket fence, Reverend McGeever came out to talk to him. "It's looking good," he said. "It's great to have you around the place."

"I'm not an expert," Matt replied, "but I do what I can. There's still a lot that needs to be done."

"Some of it can wait," the reverend said. "The old place has lasted this long, it'll last a while longer yet."

"Those joists won't," Matt replied, gesturing toward the roof. "A few have dry rot, others are infested with woodworm. We don't get that treated, the whole thing could cave in at any moment."

"Oh Matty, Matty," the reverend said, placing an arm around his shoulders. "Must you be so dramatic?"

"I just—"

"Look, I've been watching you at service, singing every song, mouthing every word."

Matt nodded. Reciting the verses was another way to keep the drink at bay. One of the members of his AA group had suggested it to him. Memorizing lines from a long text keeps the mind busy.

"Yeah, I do that."

"Not many can," the reverend said. "Look, Matt, why don't you give the sermon this weekend. I think you'd do a great job."

"Me?" Matt replied, almost dropping his brush. "You want me to do what?"

"Take the sermon. You've got a way. The people like you. When you speak after the service, people listen to you. You're a natural born leader, Matt. I can see that. Your time in the military has instilled that in you."

"Shooting a gun is one thing, Reverend, but speaking in front of a hundred people, that's a whole different ball game."

The reverend turned to him. "You can do it, son. I know you can. You'll have the Lord at your side."

Matt spent the next few days figuring out what he was going to say. He knew the reverend was trying to help him, to give him something to focus on, but actually, it was having the opposite effect. Yelling at a platoon to head into a village and take out a squad of insurgents was easy. People weren't hanging on your every word on a battlefield. They wanted to know what needed to be done, short and sharp orders with clarity. However, speaking from the heart, relaying God's word, instilling in people some joy, some hope, that was terrifying.

He researched the good book, thumbing through the pages like dollar bills, searching for inspiration, for something that made sense and gave some context to how he felt. He drank copious amounts of coffee, ate more pizza than was healthy for a man of his age, and worked out until his body ached and his joints became stiff and painful.

Friday came and went, and Saturday was a blur. He'd written everything down in handwriting that was as neat as he could muster, but he'd torn it up and started again. Now, he felt like he was about as ill prepared as he could be. For the first time since he'd found the church again, he wanted to be anywhere but there.

He stood inside, watching as the room filled with people. The Blossom family with their two sons. Old man Carter with his cane and trilby hat. The young couple from out of town who traveled thirty miles every week just to listen to Reverend McGeever's words of profound wisdom. He felt like a fraud, an understudy.

Then, he saw *her*. Blond hair, shoulder length, a petite face, small mouth, pink lips, a dash of color on her cheeks. Slim waist, eyes the color of emeralds, and tiny feet. Her delicate hands held onto a young girl, a carbon copy of her mother, maybe 10 years old, perhaps a little older.

He hadn't seen her before, he was sure of that. He would have remembered her. He thought she must be new to the church, perhaps new to the area. There was an aura that surrounded her. A happiness, joyfulness, a kind smile. He suddenly felt a sense of calmness, as if he were an aircraft coming in to land. She had done that to him without even uttering a word.

Their eyes met and she smiled. It caught him off guard and he dropped his speech, sending paper all over the floor at his feet. As he frantically collected the notecards, trying to put them back in some sort of order, he caught her laughing, but it wasn't cruel. It was if she understood him, as if she knew how he was feeling. He laughed back, and that was when they made a connection.

"The lord says that we should love one another unconditionally," he began. "We should be good to one another. Love thy neighbor. Do unto others as you would have others do to you. These are all great words; but I can tell you this, people, there have been days. Days when I could just hide myself away, lock the door, and never see another person for as long as I drew breath."

"We've all been there, right? Or, if you haven't, you know someone who has. Sometimes, things can pile on top of you. Sometimes, life can hit you so hard, it knocks the wind out of you. Sometimes, you just don't want to get out of bed." There was a murmur from the crowd, a muted agreement. "I was a soldier in the US Army. Spent my time out there in the desert, protecting our great country, doing what I thought was right. Did my time, came home, and learned how hard it is to forget, to let the horrors go. Sometimes, your present doesn't want to become your past and it lays siege to your home, kicking down the door, shaking the windows, and making sure you don't forget it."

He glanced up at the woman with the blond hair. She seemed to be hanging on his every word.

"I let those things get to me for a long time. I lost a lot of people along the way, upset those who were close to me, made some mistakes, and took my knocks. I know there's many of you in that same boat, trying to navigate those same waters, just as our lord and savior Jesus Christ did when he walked the streets of Nazarath. But that doesn't mean we should give up. We should never give up."

"Amen!" some of the congregation yelled.

"We are a community of God. We are a collection of souls who want just one thing. We want love."

"Amen!"

"We want to feel love, we want to truly experience it, to let it take over our bodies and wash away all the bad and angry feelings, the feelings of loneliness, dejection, and desperation."

"Praise the Lord!"

"But, above all, we want to give love. We want someone to devote ourselves to. We want someone to care for, to nurture, to cherish."

"Amen to that!"

"And we want to be saved, just as our lord was saved, and just as he lay down his mortal life to save every...single....one.....*of us*!"

The congregation stood and applauded as Matt held his arms aloft, reveling in the celebration. He glanced at Reverend McGeever, who was grinning and clapping his hands. The woman with the blond hair was standing, applauding, and smiling. Her eyes were on him, focused and attentive.

In that moment, he felt something he hadn't felt in such a long time. He felt like he mattered, as if he had something to offer the world. Above all, he felt like he'd given a penance and it had been accepted in some small way. He'd spoken from the heart and people had listened.

From that day forward, he never looked back.

CHAPTER ELEVEN

The Sermon

After that day, Matt found himself giving more and more sermons, and more and more people applauded. The congregation grew in size, and people traveled from miles around to come and hear the ex-soldier speak with brutal honesty about everything he had gone through, and about how the Lord had helped him get through it all. He was surprised to learn that his was a story that connected with people, that gave them hope, something to cling onto. It seemed that hope was all they wanted.

She came every time, sitting in the same spot, in the middle aisle, her daughter beside her, watching him with those brilliant green eyes and a smile that cut through his hard exterior like armor piercing bullets.

"Hi," he said. It was maybe a month after he'd first laid eyes on her, but it felt like he knew her. "Thanks for coming back again."

"I wouldn't miss it," she said. Her voice was like chocolate, smooth and warm. "My daughter and I, we love listening to you."

"I don't know about that," he said, watching as the church emptied. "I just say how I'm feeling. It don't take much."

"But that's all people want—some honesty. There's not enough truth in the world, if you ask me."

"Yeah, I guess you could say that. Names's Matt," he said. "Matt Groover."

"I know."

"Ah, yeah, sure," he replied, realizing he announced his name before every sermon.

"I'm Lyndsey, and this is my daughter Anna Jayne. We call her A.J. for short."

"Nice to meet you A.J." Matt said. "And you too, Lyndsey."

The girl tugged on her mother's arm. "Mom, you said we'd get hot chocolate after the service."

"A.J." Lyndsey blushed. "I'm talking here."

"But you said."

"That's okay," Matt interjected. "It's fine. Hey," a thought occurred to him. "I could use a lil' coffee myself, and I know a great place if you don't mind me joining you, that is."

Lyndsey glanced at her daughter. "What do you think?"

"Do they serve hot chocolate?"

Matt smiled. "Sure do. The best hot chocolate this side of Tennessee."

He sat in the coffee shop, watching as A.J. spooned mouthfuls of marshmallow and cream into her mouth. He dropped two spoonfuls of sugar in his coffee and swirled it. Across from him, Lyndsey sipped her drink. She was the most beautiful thing he'd ever seen, but she was the opposite of Tiffany, as if she wasn't trying too hard.

Lyndsey oozed class with an aura of calm, as if nothing could phase her. Her eyes reflected the sunshine, her mouth small but full, her golden hair just long enough to slip across her shoulders.

"I'm so glad you enjoy the sermons," he said. "It means the world to me."

"You're very good at it," she said, smiling. "After that first time, A.J. here half begged me to bring her back."

"Because of the hot chocolate?" he winked.

"She said you made her laugh."

He smiled at that. "Laughing with me or at me."

A.J. looked up. "A bit of both."

"Anna Jayne!" her mother cried.

"It's okay," Matt said, laughing. "If it means you keep coming back, I won't judge."

They sat there for an hour, just talking about who they were, where they'd come from. With A.J. there, Matt chose to skip the more harrowing parts, choosing instead to focus on his reconnection with God and how he and the reverend had started to build something at the Church of the Holy Saint.

"He's lucky to have you," she said. "The congregation loves you, anyone can see that. You have a way with people."

"I see it the other way," he replied. "I was cut adrift before I met the reverend. I'd hit a really low point—like way, way low. He threw me a lifeline. He didn't need to do that."

"Actually, that's kind of his job," A.J. said, spooning the last of her marshmallows from her glass. "That's what they do."

"Well, I suppose you're right. But it was the way he did it, giving me a job at first and then gradually letting my confidence build back up again until I was ready to, well, to do what I'm doing now."

"Well, whatever he did, you seem to have really taken on the role with gusto."

"Well, I thank you for saying so." The waitress came by and topped up their coffee cups. "Anyway, that's enough about me. What about you?"

Lyndsey seemed to shy away from the question. Her cheeks flushed pink, and A.J. looked up at her over the rim of her glass. "Oh, there's not really much to tell."

"Hey, you don't get to dodge the question like that."

"I'm not really great at talking about myself."

"Oh, come on now. We're all friends here."

"Look, we just met, and—" she stood. "Thanks so much for the coffee and the hot chocolate, but we really need to be on our way."

Matt looked up at her, wondering what the hell he'd said. "Oh, okay. Look, Lyndsey, if I—"

"No, really, it's fine," she helped A.J. with her coat and threw on her own. "It's no problem."

He stood. "Okay then. See you at the next sermon?"

"Wouldn't miss it for the world," she said, before hastily exiting.

Matt sat back down, nursing his bruised ego, as he watched her drive away. He'd upset her, which seemed to be on par for the course these days, but he had no idea what he'd done. He thought of her pristine appearance, of the way she held herself, the confidence in her aura, but then how that had all seemed to unravel when he asked her about her past. It had been odd, as if he'd just thrown in an emotional hand grenade. A.J. had appeared unsettled, too, as if she were worried.

He swore he'd make it up to Lyndsey when he saw her next. *He had to fix this. He just had to.*

The days went by and he counted them down, knowing that his next opportunity to see Lyndsey was at his Sunday sermon. The week seemed to drag, as if some invisible force was holding back time, preventing it from making its usual steady progress. He painted the window frames of the church, repaired a cracked pane, worked on the heating system, which was antiquated to say the least, and helped the reverend with social gatherings in the evening.

He threw himself into everything, hoping that with each good deed, he was earning himself credits in the eyes of the lord. He'd felt a connection with Lyndsey, and he couldn't get her out of his head. She was everything he was looking for and more. The weekend came and he worked on his sermon, trying to make it the best that it could be, knowing there was a distinct possibility that it was his one shot at making things right.

That Sunday, he stood at the pulpit, watching as the room began to fill. It was going to be a busy one. In less than 10 minutes, most of the seats were taken and the standing section at the back of the room was three deep.

"I must say, Matt," the reverend said. "At this rate, we're going to need a bigger church."

Matt nodded his head, but his eyes never left the room. He was looking for her, hoping and praying that she would come walking through that door, her eyes bright and alert, A.J. standing beside her.

Time passed, and as the seconds became minutes, he began to realize one unmistakable truth: She wasn't coming. He'd driven her away. He had a room full of people, but the one person he wanted there more than anyone else was going to stay away, perhaps for good.

"Time to start," the reverend said, checking his watch. "When you're ready, Matt. You may as well begin."

The sermon was fine. He'd written it out and rehearsed it over a dozen times that morning, but with Lyndsey not there, he just couldn't bring himself to deliver it with the same level of passion and emotion. The audience noticed it, too, and he spotted a few at the back of the room trying to slip away unnoticed.

As he gave the usual handshakes and "thank you's" to the departing congregation at the end of the session, he sensed most of them knew something was off. He tried to give off his usual confident air, but he just knew it wasn't cutting it. Nobody was getting fooled, least of all himself.

"Everything okay, Matthew?" the reverend asked when they were alone. "You don't seem yourself, son."

Matt thought of the seats where Lyndsey and A.J. usually sat, their places taken by an elderly couple from downtown.

"Yeah, fine," he said. "A few things on my mind, is all."

The reverend unfastened the top button of his shirt. "In my experience, that usually means a woman's involved." Matt didn't reply, just scratched at his whiskers. "Yes, I thought as much. The lady with the blond hair and young daughter, I'm guessing." Matt looked up. He had no idea how the reverend could have known that. "She's new to our flock," the reverend continued "She'd visited with her daughter a few times before you arrived, but not often. I sense there's trouble in her past."

Matt cocked his head. "How do you mean?"

"I have a knack for these types of things, Matt. You might say I have God's ear. I listen to the way people are, just as I listened when you showed up, looking up at the church as if it was your only hope of salvation."

"I guess it was," Matt said.

"And she has a similar look, except she's got someone to look out for, as well as herself. That makes her plight a little more complicated."

Matt thought of Tiffany and the son he would never know, realizing that he would never understand that level of responsibility, the eternal burden, that weighed heavily on a parent's shoulders. He instantly felt regret, knowing that his downfall was his own to bear.

"I thought we had a connection, you know?" he said, wondering if he sounded as stupid as he felt.

"Then my advice is hold tight, my friend. If she feels the same way, she'll be back."

Matt wondered if the reverend was right, if he was really as in tune with people's thoughts and feelings as he thought he was. The fact was, sometimes people let you down, and sometimes shit happened. There was just no getting away from it.

Chapter Twelve

Moving On

"It's about Dad," Marshall said, sounding about as anxious as Matt had ever heard him. "He's been involved in an incident."

"What kind of incident?" Matt replied, not wanting to think about the man who no longer claimed to be his father.

"A bad one."

"I'm not following."

There was a heavy sigh on the end of the line. "Apparently, an inmate took a dislike to what Dad did to Mom and he was attacked while he was waiting in line for dinner. He's in the ICU."

Matt let the news wash over him, not knowing if he should feel joy or anger that he hadn't been able to give the punishment himself.

"What do you want me to do about it?"

"He's dying, Matt," Marshall said. "Doctors have got him stabilized, but his heart's not up to the job of keeping him alive. He's already had two cardiac arrests, and they think a third will finish him off."

Good, Matt thought. *Let the fucker die alone with no one caring whether he pulls through.*

"What do you want me to do with this information, Marshall?" he sniped, his voice thin and bitter.

"I don't know, I—"

"You know he's not my dad, right? You know mom wasn't my mom, you're not my brother? In fact, I'm not related to any of you. I'm a baby in a basket, abandoned by his family for the price of a handshake and a couple of baggies."

"What?! No. I don't believe that."

"Believe what you will, but that's what the old man told me."

"Matt, that's not—"

"So forgive me if I'm struggling to care here," he said. "It's just, that man beat the living crap out of me, killed the woman I thought was my mom, and then told me my whole life had been a lie. Kind of leaves a bad taste in the mouth."

The line went silent, and for a moment Matt thought his brother had hung up, not wanting to face such a bitter truth. "Matt, I'm so sorry."

"Don't be," he said, relishing the anger, absorbing the spite. "I've moved on."

That afternoon, Matt sat in the coffee shop, nursing his third cup, hoping the caffeine satisfied at least some of his intense, burning desire to head down to a bar and down the first bottle of Jack he came across. *God's with me*, he repeated over and over in his head. *God is helping me.* He hoped for his own sake that He was, because if He wasn't, Matt knew he had a date with the patron saint of liquor.

The call came through while he watched the sun slowly setting on the horizon. It was his brother's number, and he knew that could only mean one thing. As he raised his cell phone to his ear and hit the receive button, she pulled into the parking lot, her red Prius unmistakeable with the tiny dent on the front fender.

"He's gone," Marshall said as she opened the door. "He's dead."

Matt raised a hand and waved as she spotted him. "Okay."

"You want to see him before they take the body away?"

Lyndsey opened the door, and, all of a sudden, Matt felt like an enormous weight had been lifted from his shoulders.

"Marshall," he said as she walked over, smelling of sunshine and berries. "*Let that fucker burn.*"

He placed the phone on the table and stood, holding out his hand. She took it and they embraced. The warmth of her skin against his was like an antidote to him.

"Are you okay?" she asked as she sat down. "You look like you've seen a ghost."

"Not one that I'm afraid of," he said. "Not anymore." She ordered a coffee and a slice of apple pie, and he followed suit. "How did you find me here?" he asked as the waitress cleaned their table.

"It was the last place I saw you, so I took a chance. I'm sorry we missed the service."

"Not one of my better ones," he replied.

"You spooked me a little the other day. I needed time to think."

Matt let those words sink in. If she needed time to think, that meant there was something she wasn't telling him.

"Are you in some sort of trouble?" he asked. "Because if you are, I can help."

"No, nothing like that." The pie arrived and they paused their conversation, waiting for the waitress to bring over the coffees.

"Is A.J. okay?"

"Yes. She's at a sleepover with her friend. She's perfectly fine." She ate some of her pie, chewing slowly, watching him. Matt thought she looked nervous and unsettled, as if there was something playing on her mind. He decided not to push it.

"How's your pie?"

"My husband was a criminal," she said. "A bad one."

Her words surprised Matt, and he set down his fork. "Alright."

"Just let me get this out," she said. "Because I've been thinking about how I reacted the other day, and I think I reacted that way because I was afraid to tell you everything. I know that sounds stupid, especially because I haven't done anything wrong. A.J. and I, we're the victims, along with so many other people, but—I don't know—maybe it's just the shame."

Matt reached out and took her hand, curling his coarse fingers into her tiny palms. "You don't need to do this. If it makes you uncomfortable, you don't need to say anything."

"No, I want to." The guy on the next table was looking on and Matt shot him a glare that said, *Look away, friend, or you'll find yourself wishing you'd taken your coffee someplace else.* With that, the guy stood up and hastily departed, leaving them alone. "We lived in Dallas for a while," she said. "That was where I met him. I was working in his building, and he would come and go, sometimes buy me a coffee. He was charming."

Matt noted the irony, but didn't mention it.

"We dated for a few months. I didn't know who he was or what he did, just that he was involved in property development. He seemed like a nice guy. Anyway, things started to progress and he took me to meet his family. I should have known right away what I was getting myself into, but maybe I had the new relationship bug, I don't know. They had a certain way, you know? Like you see in the movies? They didn't have real jobs like you or me. They did construction work, they owned property, they dealt in shipping and logistics. None of it seemed legitimate."

Matt knew where she was heading with this. "So, they were a crime family?"

"Something like that. I like to think I wasn't seduced by the money, but when I lay awake at night, thinking about what happened, I wonder if I was. Before I knew it, we were married, and not long after that I fell pregnant with A.J."

"Sounds a little rushed."

"It was," she replied, seemingly happy that he'd noticed. "It was his idea, like if we didn't do it right away, he'd lose me or something. My mom was dead against it. She knew something was off right from the get go, but I didn't listen.

"Anyway, after Anna Jayne arrived, things started to go wrong. He'd be gone for days, I wouldn't hear from him, and when I did, he'd be tired and anxious. It was almost as if he thought that someone was coming for him."

"Maybe they were," he said.

"Yeah. Well, on A.J.'s first birthday, we had a little get together at our place, except Mason, A.J.'s father, never showed up. In fact, he didn't show up at all that week. His father, understandably, was worried, and he sent a few of his goons to find him. The next thing I know, we're visiting Mason in hospital. He was so coked up out of his mind that he didn't know who we were or where he was."

Matt had heard the story a million times, and he instantly wanted to do something for Lyndsey to help her. She'd clearly been terrified of this man, and had done everything she could to protect her daughter.

"I found out he'd been seeing at least two other women behind my back and blowing our money on a drug and gambling habit that would put Tiger Woods to shame. We were in debt up to our eyeballs. His father stepped in and settled the debt, of course, but that didn't stop Mason. Once he was out of hospital, he went straight back to it, and that was when I decided to leave."

"Except he wouldn't let you," Matt said.

She nodded, glaring at her pie. "He never hit me, but he was about as nasty as he could be. He called me every name you could think of and questioned my ability to raise our daughter." Matt averted his gaze, recalling the way he had spoken to Tiffany. "I was too terrified of him to walk out, so I stayed. I feel ashamed saying that now, but you have to believe me, I was genuinely in fear of my life."

Matt shook his head. "You have nothing to be ashamed of. How did you get away?"

"I didn't," she said. "Not for a long time, years. I just found a way to get by, to ignore everything that was going on around me—the shady deals, the violence, the betrayals. When I look back at that time, I could barely remember who I was or what I'd become. It was like I was living another life, as if I wasn't in my own mind."

"It must have been awful."

"It was."

"But you're here now, so what happened?"

She paused to consider her answer. "Fate intervened."

"I don't understand," Matt said.

"Turns out Mason was in debt to the wrong people—people even his own family couldn't protect him against. The police found his body in the trunk of a car after an anonymous tip. They'd cut out his eyeballs before slitting his throat. It was a message."

"Wow," Matt said. "I'm so sorry."

"Don't be. They did me a favor." She shook her head, blushing. "That sounds so awful, doesn't it? I know he was A.J.'s father, but he wasn't, not really. We didn't see him for weeks at a time. When he was home, he wasn't really there. A.J. didn't really know him at all."

Matt knew that feeling well. A fleeting memory of the man he had called his dad flashed through his mind, and it wasn't a pleasant one. Then, he remembered he was dead. The man who had caused him so much pain was no more. He wondered if his lack of emotion was symptomatic of something deeper, but he doubted it. He hated him.

"Are you okay?" Lyndsey asked. "I think I lost you there."

"I'm fine," he said. "I'm just thinking about your story. When did you decide to get out?"

"Straight away," she said. "It was the push I needed. I spoke to my mom and told her I needed to leave town. She understood completely. She'd wanted me to get out for years."

"What about his family?"

"They were knee-deep in a gang war. The last thing on their mind was what their son's miserable widow was up to. We just caught the next flight out of town, which brought us here."

He pushed his unfinished pie away and took her hand once more. "I'm sorry for what you went through. You and A.J. That wasn't fair on you."

"Life's not fair," she said, dabbing at her eyes. "But sometimes you have to go through hard times to make it through to the other side, to find something better."

She gripped his hands tightly, as if she was afraid to let go. Her story had caught him off guard; it wasn't what he had expected at all, but it made her even more appealing to him. They had both had their fair share of troubles, and they had earned their scars. She had been through hell, and so had he; and while he was still staggering and stumbling his way through life, she had walked out the other side with her head held high. She had a strength that he could only admire. Sure, he had fought on the battlefields of Iraq, had led soldiers to countless military victories, had lost friends and colleagues for a war he didn't truly understand, but this woman with the golden hair and emerald green eyes had endured a torment and mental torture that would have destroyed men twice her size. She was a force of nature, and that made her even more attractive.

"Why did you come here, Lyndsey?" he asked, "Aside from the good company, I mean."

She peered down at their hands, her petite fingers laced inside his strong grip. They could have been a married couple sitting there, discussing their day like a million others.

"I wanted to see you," she said. "And to tell you why I left in such a hurry. I wanted you to understand."

"I do understand," he replied, thinking of his father's dead body lying on a gurney, bruised and beaten, his heart a ruptured piece of decomposing tissue in his chest. "More than you'll ever know."

CHAPTER THIRTEEN

The Next Flight

That conversation was the icebreaker, a moment that changed Matt's life forever. He was a man reborn. Lyndsey and A.J. provided him with a purpose, a focal point for everything that was to come. It felt like a bitter irony that the day he finally figured out where he was headed, his dad passed in the most violent of circumstances. *Maybe,* he thought, *it was bitter justice, coupled with his own personal reinvention.* And, if anyone needed reinventing, it was him.

For their first proper date, he took Lyndsey to an Italian restaurant in the center of town, followed by a movie. It all felt so surreal to him, as if it was all an out of body experience. It didn't seem so long ago that he was in the desert, eating chow with the guys and wondering what the next day would bring. Eating pasta and clams and looking forward to Keanu Reeve's next big budget action movie just didn't feel normal to him.

What did feel normal, and about as comfortable as pulling on an old pair of jeans, was talking to Lyndsey. It felt natural, easy, maybe even calming. She had such a relaxed demeanor, which was surprising given what she'd told him about her past. Nothing seemed to phase her, not even when he told her about what happened to his mom and best friend, and how his ex had taken his unborn son away from him.

"Will you go looking for them?" she asked in the bar after the movie, sipping a Martini. "Your ex and your son, I mean."

He shook his head. "She made a very convincing argument for why I shouldn't, and the worst thing is, I think she was right."

"About you being bad for them?"

"And about her new life being good for the boy. I couldn't hope to give him what her new partner could, and I wouldn't want to be the one to spoil everything for him."

"You wouldn't. You're not the same person you used to be, the one you told me about."

He sipped his Pepsi and eyed the rows of liquor bottles that lined the shelves behind the bar. "I'm always one bad decision away from being that person again," he said. "And she knows that."

She looked stunning, dressed in a red button-up blouse with loose fitting, black pants. Her hair hung to her shoulders, and her lips and nails were painted pink. She smelled great too, woody with a hint of berries, and her high heeled shoes sparkled as she walked.

"I love being with you," he said.

"You too," she replied, sipping her drink. "I feel like we've known each other forever."

Matt knew what she meant. It was almost as if they'd been friends since kindergarten. He knew what she was going to say almost before she said it, and he could sense when she was happy or when she was feeling anxious. It was like they were in sync in some telepathic way. He'd never felt that way before with any woman. Not with any of his girlfriends prior to the war, and certainly not with Tiffany. It was a new sensation to him, and one that he liked a lot.

"I'll take you home," he said, noticing the time. "I'm guessing you need to get back to A.J."

"Actually," she replied, touching his hand. "She's at a sleepover with a friend. My apartment is empty."

Matt walked her home, taking the scenic route and enjoying the night air. They talked the whole way there, laughing and joking, but Matt's mind was on what was to come. His past few relationships had been all about the sex, but this thing with Lyndsey was something different entirely. This meant something. This was something he couldn't afford to mess up.

With the apartment door shut behind them, he pulled Lyndsey close, kissing her. Her tongue probed his, soft but urgent.

"Are you sure you want to do this?" he asked, every fiber of his body hoping she would say yes.

"I do," she said, her fingers running through his hair. "I really do."

They fell into the bedroom, pulling at each others' clothes, tossing the bed sheets onto the floor. The sex was fantastic, slow and tender. They explored each other's bodies, her hands pausing only to feel the scars in his biceps and across his chest. Her body was firm yet supple, and her skin was like silk.

When it was done, they lay in each others' arms, breathless and covered in a thin sheen of sweat. The light from the full moon seeped through a crack in the drapes, revealing their bodies in its milky white glow.

"I don't want this to be it," she said. "I want to see you again."

He sat up and looked down at her, drawing his hand across her toned stomach. "Me too," he said. "This feels real to me. I wanted you as soon as I laid eyes on you. When I thought you'd run out on me, I didn't know what I was going to do."

She ran her finger down his spine. "I'll never do that again. I promise."

"You'd better not."

She made them coffee and they sat up, talking and laughing. They spoke about the church, about Matt's relationship with the reverend, and whether Lyndsey thought Mason's family would come looking for her and A.J.

She shook her head. "I don't think they will. They knew what he put me through and they didn't do anything to help me. I think they're too ashamed to seek me out."

"I hope you're right."

"Me too."

As he sipped his coffee, a thought occurred to him. "What about your mom?"

"What about her?"

"Don't you want to see her?"

"Well, yeah, but I've been so busy setting up my new life here that—" she paused. "I don't know. It would be good to see her again, I guess. I know A.J. would love to be with her again."

Matt stood and placed his cup in the sink. "Well, if you wouldn't mind an old soldier like me tagging along, then I'd be happy to pay for the airline tickets."

She laughed and kissed him. "I might just take you up on that." She squeezed his arm and ran her hand down his naked skin. "But, before we do that, let's see if the first time was just luck."

He laughed, sweeping her up into his arms and carrying her into the bedroom. "Oh, I can assure you, Lil' Miss, luck had nothing to do with it."

That night, he dreamed of Kenzo lying dead in the sand, bullets fizzing past his head like fireflies. He ducked behind the humvee, his rifle pulled across his chest, and listened as the bullets ricocheted off its metal exterior. To his left, there was an explosion, and one of his colleagues was ripped to pieces, his limbs tossed in all directions as blood splattered across the battlefield. Another one of his platoon took shrapnel to his face, tearing a hole in his cheek as big as a baseball. He dropped to the ground, an eyeball hanging from the socket like a stone in a sock.

"Help me," he said. "Matt, get me outta here."

He stood and returned fire, but there were way too many of them. They had them surrounded. The noise of gunfire seemed to last forever, like someone rattling a chain. The roar of IEDs as they detonated was deafening. He dropped to his knees, his rifle crashing to the ground, and he watched as the Iraqis came at him, their knives drawn, their mouths pulled down in vicious snarls.

"Okay," he said. "I'm ready. Take me, I'm ready." The first Iraqi was upon him, his weapon raised. "Come on, you fucker!" Matt roared. "What are you waiting for?"

"Matt, Matt," a woman's voice whispered from another universe.

"No!" he cried. "Leave me alone, leave me alone!"

There were hands on his shoulders, and a woman's lips on his cheek.

"Matt, it's me, Lyndsey. Wake up."

He opened his eyes, but everything was a blur. He appeared to be sitting upright, his legs over the edge of the bed. The woman was next to him. It seemed like she was trying to soothe him.

"I'm sorry," he said. "I'm so, so sorry."

"What for?"

"I killed them," he replied. "I killed all of them."

She pulled him into her arms and ran her hands through her hair. He was confused and disorientated, but slowly he began to remember where he was and who he was with. The room seemed more and more familiar to him, as did the bed and the smell of Lyndsey's sweet perfume.

Once he'd calmed down, they sat and talked.

"How long have you been having those?" she asked.

"The nightmares?" She nodded. "Since maybe three or four months into my first tour. You kind of get used to them."

"You shouldn't have to."

"Well, up until now it's only really been me who they've affected."

She gripped his hand. "You know, maybe seeing someone about the way you feel, about your PTSD—which is what I think you have—perhaps that will help you."

He thought of Chris and the way he had looked, lying there on the floor with two holes in his head and his brains on the walls. He didn't want to be like him, but he also didn't know if he could sit with someone and recount the horrors he'd witnessed.

"Yeah, I don't really do that. I don't think it will help."

"Well, one thing's for sure. Bottling it all up is certainly not going to." He knew she was right, but he'd coped with the nightmares and the visions for so long that they were almost comforting to him. They were like home, almost as if he needed to feel the suffering to get some sense of himself. "Look," she said. "I know someone. She's an expert at this type of thing. She's dealt with dozens of ex-soldiers before, and each one has given her a glowing recommendation. As luck would have it, her office is in Pennsylvania, no more than a few miles away from my mom's place."

Matt started to feel like he was being maneuvered into a position he didn't want to be in. "I'll think about it."

"Sure, but don't leave this, Matt. Stuff like this can really escalate if left untreated."

He saw the blood on the walls again, Kenzo lying dying in the street, the sound of Sue's sobs as she sat slumped on the sofa. "Look, I said I'd think about it, okay?!"

Lyndsey's hands stopped moving up and down his spine, and she exhaled loudly. "I was only trying to help."

She stood and went to the bathroom, and he sat alone on the bed, looking at his reflection in the mirror. He was a big guy with a thick beard, dark eyes, scars that mottled his body, and pronounced muscles in his arms and chest. To an outsider, he was the typical hard man with a stern exterior, hardened expression, and the physique that went with it. However, inside he felt broken, battered by everything that had happened to him. Was he really going to let some misguided sense of self protection stop him from opening up to the one woman in his life who seemed to make it all make sense? If that was the way he was going to act, he deserved what was coming to him, and none of it was good.

He went to the door and tapped lightly. "You okay in there?" he asked.

"Yeah, I'm fine."

"Look, I'm sorry I snapped."

She opened the door. She'd been crying. "It's no problem. Who am I to tell you what to do with your life? We've really only just met, and—" she touched his hand. "Look, I do this. I try to fix people, even though I couldn't fix my own marriage. You've every right to tell me to go to hell."

He pulled her into his strong arms and held her close. "I would never do that. And you're right, I do need help."

She peered up at him. "You're sure?"

"If this friend of yours can make me feel normal, whatever that is," he said, smiling, "then I say, let's get the next flight to Pennsylvania."

CHAPTER FOURTEEN

The Whirlpool

The next flight wasn't as easy to catch as they had hoped. Matt still had things to finish up at the church and A.J. still had school to attend, so they waited for the Columbus Day school holiday, which was five weeks away.

In that time, Matt spent the majority of his time with Lyndsey and her daughter, rarely going back to his own apartment. The place held bad memories for him, after all. He'd been a shell of himself there, drinking himself into a hole he couldn't climb out of, and wrecking the relationship he had with the mother of a child he would never get to see.

He and Lyndsey grew so close, so fast, that it was almost scary. Matt had never fallen so quickly before, but that was how he felt.

The nightmares continued, as did the depression that caught him off guard from time to time, slapping him across the face with a wet palm and reminding him that it was still there, lurking in the darkness and waiting for him to let his guard down. Knowing he was going to see someone who had experience with this kind of thing gave him hope, and it was the hope that kept him going. Lyndsey had been right about one thing: He needed fixing, alright.

They did things he had never done before, like spend family days at the zoo and the amusement park, riding roller coasters and ferris wheels, eating cotton candy, and shooting ducks out of a barrel. He'd never had kids, so he had nothing to compare it to, but he guessed that the way he felt about A.J. was as close to the way he would feel about a daughter of his own.

"I think she likes you," Lyndsey said as they walked home from the park, arm in arm, as A.J. raced ahead.

"I like her, too. She's a good kid."

"She's had a tough time of it, you know."

"Yeah, I get that."

"She's never really had a father to look up to. Mason was never there for her. For either of us."

Matt liked the feeling of responsibility that being a de facto parent brought with it. He hadn't expected to inherit a kid just as he was losing his own, but he found he had a knack for it, even though he'd had no role model to teach him.

"Well, everyone needs two parents in their lives, that's what I think. And if I can even get close to being the father she needs, then I would be pretty happy."

He didn't know if he even had what it took, realizing he had so much hatred for his own dad, but he hoped he could suppress that and give A.J. the upbringing she deserved.

Lyndsey turned to face him and reached up to kiss him. "You're a good man, Matt Groover. You know that, right?"

He smiled and kissed her back, hoping he could be. "Well, I do my best."

With the flights booked, Matt and Lyndsey sat down to tell A.J. the good news. Lyndsey served up meatloaf and mashed potato, with a side salad you could dive right into.

"You remember your nana?" Lyndsey asked, spooning potatoes onto her daughter's plate. "My mom. Nana Lizzie?"

"Sure do," A.J. replied. "I love Nana Lizzie. She makes the best cakes in the whole world. This one time," she said excitedly, turning to Matt, "she made chocolate cake with vanilla frosting—and she put raspberry jelly *right in the middle*."

"Sounds great," Matt said, thinking the whole thing sounded like a sugar rush on steroids.

"Well," Lyndsey continued. "How would you like to go and see Nana Lizzie again? See whether she can still make cakes as delicious as that?"

"Serious?" A.J. cried. "You're not messing with me, are you?" She glared at Matt and he shrugged. "You better not be."

"Your mom said I could tag along," he said. "Would that be okay?"

"Do you know my nana?"

The question took Matt by surprise. "Well, no, but—"

"Matt's got some business in Pennsylvania," Lyndsey interjected. "So, he's going to come with us. Nana said we can all stay over, if that's okay with you."

A.J. sized Matt up with a serious look on her face, but eventually her stern demeanor broke into a broad grin and she laughed. "Well, if Nana Lizzie says it's okay, then it's cool beans with me."

Matt glanced at Lyndsey, who's eyes were smiling, and he cracked up. "Cool beans? Where did you get that from?"

"Billy Waters at school," she said. "Says it all the time. He's such a nut." They sat and ate their dinner, talking about A.J.'s day and learning all about classroom politics, when suddenly A.J. changed the subject. "Wait a minute. Nana Lizzie lives all the way out there in Pennsylvania, which is, like, far, isn't it?"

Lyndsey nodded. "Yeah, almost 800 miles, actually."

A.J. puffed out her cheeks. "*Phew!* That's a long way."

Matt didn't think it was that far at all, but A.J. was a 10 year old kid, and to them, a three-story building was tall and a walk to the shop two blocks over could seem like a 30-mile hike.

"I'm guessing you're wondering how we're getting there?" Matt asked, knowing that A.J. had never been on an airplane before. She and her mom had traveled from Dallas to Tennessee by car.

A.J. nodded, dark gravy coating her lips.

Matt reached inside his pocket and pulled out the airplane tickets, tossing them to her. On the front, there was a picture of a 737 racing across a brilliant blue backdrop.

"No way!" she cried. "No freaking way!"

"Anna Jayne!" her mom said. "I know you're excited, but no cussing at the table."

"But it's an airplane, Mom!" she said. "A great big airplane."

"And, if you behave yourself and work hard at school, you'll see it up close in a couple of weeks." Lyndsey set down her knife and fork and folded her fingers beneath her chin.

"This is so awesome!"

"It sure is. But, honey, Matt paid for the tickets, so I think we both owe him a big thank you, don't we?"

"You did?"

"Well," Matt said. "I heard all about your Nana's cooking, so I thought it was worth it."

With that, A.J. jumped down from her chair, raced toward him, and threw her arms around his neck. "Thank you," she said, burying her face beneath his chin. "Thank you so much!"

The departure day approached faster than Matt was expecting. He was still knee-deep in paint and paintbrushes, and had barely started decorating the church's high ceiling. He stood atop a tall ladder, prepping the woodwork, when there was a voice from beneath him.

"Aintcha supposed to be heading off on a Columbus Day break?" the reverend called. "I bet you haven't even packed."

"Flights not until the morning, Reverend," Matt replied. "I got plenty of time."

"That woman's gonna string you up from the nearest tree if you miss your flight."

"Don't worry yourself, Reverend. Ain't gonna happen."

The truth was, Matt had a bad feeling about the trip, even though it was he who had encouraged Lyndsey to arrange it in the first place. He hadn't flown since coming back from overseas, and, for some strange reason, his mind was connecting this flight out of Nashville International with everything that had gone down in Iraq. It was illogical, it was nonsensical, but Lyndsey had made Matt understand that he wasn't entirely in control of his brain, and in some way, that comforted him.

He went home that night and threw some things into a suitcase, feeling anxious about the trip but looking forward to taking a holiday with the two people he now felt closer to than his own brother.

When he arrived at Lyndsey's apartment, preparations were in full swing. A.J. was already trying on some of her holiday clothes, and Lyndsey was sipping a glass of wine, listening to some pop mix on her Amazon sound system, and dancing around the room while laying various costumes out on the sofa as she seemingly tried to make sure everything was coordinated. Matt's carry-on bag looked pretty pathetic by comparison.

"Is that all you're taking?" Lyndsey asked, laughing. "Are you sure that's enough?"

"They do have shops in Pennsylvania, you know?" he replied. "If I run out of stuff, I'll just buy more."

Lyndsey's iPad let out a tinny jingling sound, and she went to it. "Hey, it's mom. She's face-timing us."

Matt didn't know much about what a "face-time" was, but he knew where the coffee was, so he poured himself a cup.

"Hi Lyndsey," came a thin, reedy voice. "Your Uncle Bob showed me how to use this thing. Is it working okay?"

Her daughter laughed. "It sure is, Mom. It's good to see your face." There were tears in Lyndsey's eyes. "We're going to be with you tomorrow, you know?"

"Yeah, I know, but I just thought I'd call to make sure you've got everything packed. I remember how absent-minded you can be. Don't forget your shampoo and your hairdryer."

Lyndsey shook her head. "It's good to see you haven't changed, Mom." She turned to Matt. "Here, I want you to meet somebody. I was going to introduce you tomorrow, but seeing as you couldn't wait—" She ushered Matt over, and he stooped to see the face of a woman with long dark hair with gray flecks scattered through it, round glasses that seemed too big for her slim face, and a thin mouth. A smile spread across her face as she took in Matt's appearance.

"Well, didn't you find yourself a big hunk of a man?" she cried. "Boy, you been eating beef steak all your life, aintcha?"

Matt grinned. "Something like that. It's nice to meet you, Mrs Carter."

"Oh, call me Lizzie," she replied, flapping a hand and shaking the screen in the process. "If you're going to be part of the family, you've got to drop the formalities."

A.J. came racing in as she heard her nanna's voice, and she almost clattered into the iPad.

"Nana Lizzie!" she yelled. "Is that you?"

"It sure is, sweetheart. Oh my, look how you've grown."

"I sure have. I'm almost as tall as Mama now."

"I bet you are, sweetheart, and you're just as pretty as a picture, too."

"We're coming to see you tomorrow, Nana. Matt's bought us tickets to ride in a great big airplane, and we're gonna land in Philadelphia, and then get in a car so we can drive right to your house."

"I know," she said. "And I just can't wait to give you a great big hug."

"Have you baked a cake?"

"Oh, darling, I've baked the biggest cake your young eyes will ever have laid eyes upon!"

"With the vanilla frosting?"

"With more vanilla frosting than you've ever seen in your whole life."

A.J. turned to face her mom. "Did you hear that, Mom? Did you hear what Nana Lizzie said?"

"I sure did," Lyndsey replied. "I sure did."

When the call ended, they sat on the couch and watched as A.J. tried to zip her case shut.

"You okay?" Lyndsey asked him. "You don't look so good."

That bad feeling was gnawing away at him, making him feel uneasy, as if something sinister was lurking just out of sight. He fought to shake it off. "Yeah, I'm fine. Just a little tired, I guess."

"You sit here," she replied. "I can finish packing, and then we can get to bed. We've got an early start in the morning, after all."

"No, it's fine. I'm sorry, I don't want to ruin the excitement."

"You're not."

"It's just, I've not been on an airplane since, you know, when I came back from Iraq. I think it's bringing things home to me."

She grabbed his hands and turned to face him. "Which is exactly why you're going to see Isobel, my psychiatrist friend. This trip is the start of a long process for you, Matt, but it's one that will make you well again, I'm sure of it."

He nodded slowly, watching as the coffee swirled around in his mug like a whirlpool sucking him down into its unseen depths. "I hope so," he said, almost hypnotized as it twisted round and around. "I really do."

CHAPTER FIFTEEN

The Uncle

They checked in early, and grabbed coffee and waffles before takeoff. A.J. had yet another hot chocolate and devoured her waffles covered in ice cream and syrup in record time. She was so excited, so in awe of the magic of flight. She gazed out the window as an Airbus A380 launched itself from the runway, and watched as the enormous metal bird turned mid air, graceful and elegant.

"It's amazing," she sighed. "How does it even work?"

"It's a little thing called aerodynamics that I'm sure they'll teach you all about in school," Matt replied.

"Basically, air is pushed over the top of the wing much faster than beneath the wing, creating something called lift."

A.J.s eyed rolled as she yawned.

"I don't think she's quite ready to become an aero engineer just yet," Lyndsey said, laughing.

"I guess not."

Matt couldn't shake his feeling that something bad was about to happen. He knew it was illogical and based on emotion rather than fact, but the feeling stayed with him. Nevertheless, like a scent he couldn't shift. He toyed with his stetson, pulling his dark denim jacket across his chest.

He glanced around the concourse, watching as hundreds of travelers dragged pull-along bags to their gate, always in a hurry, always appearing like they should have been there minutes ago. Families raced along, the parents dragging the kids who were always seemingly preoccupied with something in one of the store fronts. Business people pushed their suitcases in front of them, as if they were walking square dogs, sipping takeaway coffee and talking through earpieces that made it appear like they were speaking to themselves. Couples walked arm in arm, some arguing about which gate they were supposed to be heading to, others looking like they were racing off on a romantic getaway. Lone travelers shuffled along like zombies, appearing as though the airport was the last place they wanted to be in the whole world.

Nothing looked out of the ordinary or out of place. It was just life, and it was happening all around them.

"Are you okay, Matt?" Lyndsey asked, touching his hand. "It looked like we lost you there for a moment."

"No," he replied, shaking himself from his thoughts. "Just thinking about the trip, that's all."

"You worried about meeting my mother?"

He frowned. The woman had seemed a little full on, but he'd never been anxious about meeting people. Meeting people was the easy part. Maintaining any sort of meaningful relationship was the bit he always found more treacherous.

"Not at all. I'm looking forward to it."

"The therapy then?"

He thought about that for a moment. Sure, he was a little troubled about the whole thing, concerned that he would be forced to reveal things about himself that he would really rather keep buried. However, it wasn't playing on his mind, not as much as the notion that they were heading for some form of disaster.

"Hey, I'm fine. It's just a little early, and my social battery isn't fully charged yet."

She smiled, before glancing up at the digital screen that was hanging from the cafeteria wall.

"Hell," she said. "The gate's open. We should get moving."

"Cool!" A.J. yelled, slurping the last of the cream from her glass. "I can't wait!"

They took their seats on the right hand side of the 737, just ahead of the wings, with A.J. taking the window seat. She gazed through the glass, watching as the plane pushed off from the gate.

"It's moving, Mom," she cried. "Look, we're going backward!"

"I know, love, but try to keep it down a little. People are trying to relax."

As the pilot guided the plane to the runway, Matt felt his internal warning system triggering, telling him this was a mistake, that he should alert the cabin staff to what was going on and insist that they abort the takeoff. He thought of the moment the wheel's touched down in the desert, of the feeling that he was heading into the unknown where thousands of enemy forces were waiting for him, aiming to snuff out his life as easily as snuffing out a candle. Everything felt wrong, everything was upside down.

He thought of Tiffany and of his unborn son, growing like an orange in her womb, developing limbs and a brain, little eyes, and a mouth. They were thousands of miles away, and about to embark on a journey that he could never truly understand. *What if he never came home? What if his son never got to know him? What if he was making a terrible mistake heading to Pennsylvania with the woman he cared for so much, and a young girl he now thought of as his daughter?* Everything was so complex, so difficult to piece together. *What if the plane never touched down?*

There was a loud roar as the jet engines sprang to life, and Matt glared out the window as the ground started to move beneath them. Slowly at first, and then faster, the asphalt whistled past at frightening speed.

A.J.'s expression darkened as she gripped the arms of her chair. She suddenly seemed less excited about being thrown into the air in a steel tube at 500 miles an hour, climbing to 35,000 feet. Lyndsay gripped his hand and smiled. She looked about as happy as he'd ever seen her. They were traveling as a family. She had left behind a life that had dealt her so many blows, and she was speeding toward a new one with a man she loved and a daughter she would give her life for.

Once they reached altitude and the seatbelt sign was turned off, Matt stood. He needed the mens' room, but more than that, he needed to shake off the remnants of his anxiety. Taking off safely had helped settle his notion that something disastrous was about to happen, but that didn't mean he was fully at ease. It still lingered, the dread, like a bug that kept slapping into his cheek.

The queue was about three deep, and he stood at the back of the plane, watching as people shuffled about in their seats and the cabin staff tried to deliver beverages to those who wanted it. It was the rude people who annoyed him, the self-entitled, those who seemed like their status was like a tattoo—it could never be erased. These people had never seen suffering, never had to scrape by on what little they could afford, had never fought a war. He found himself almost wishing for the great leveler—something that would take away everything these people had, leaving them penniless and wondering where their next meal was going to come from. *How would they behave then? How would they treat their neighbors?*

The door to the men's room opened and he stepped inside, pulling the door closed behind him and sitting on the toilet seat, breathing deeply. Perhaps it was the altitude, but he was feeling agitated. People were getting to him. All the pushing and shoving and angry looks. *What was it with people? Where did they get off looking at him like that?*

He sat there for a few minutes, trying to calm himself. He knew his PTSD had been triggered, but he didn't know how he could pull himself back out of it. He didn't want to upset Lyndsey and A.J., so keeping himself away from them seemed like the better option for everybody.

There was a tap at the door.

"You going to be much longer in there?"

He felt his body tense. "Gonna be as long as I need to be. Try the next one along."

"That's occupied too. Look, buddy, I need to take a shit and you've been in there long enough already."

"I said I'm not done yet, pal. Just cool it, wontcha?"

"Jeez," he heard the man say. "Are you listening to this guy?"

Matt closed his eyes and focused on the positives. He was with a woman he was slowly falling in love with, a kid who made him smile. He had a good job back at the church, and a friend in Reverend McGeever. He had a lot to look forward to, if only he could get himself together, and Lyndsey was helping out with that, too. *Focus*, he whispered to himself, *just be the best person you can be.*

He stood and glared at himself in the mirror, wondering where all the lines had come from and when the gray flecks in his hair and beard had emerged. Life was passing him by and he needed to take control of it. He needed to steer the ship.

Tap, tap.

"Come on, man. You must be done in there."

Matt opened the door and peered down at the small guy with the thin lips. He stifled a growl as the man backed away.

"Sorry about that," Matt said. "Must have been the clams."

The man pushed past him without saying a word, but Matt decided not to react, despite his desire to grab the man by the throat and throw him against the wall. Lyndsey needed him to be better than that, and so did he.

He walked along the aisle, trying to avoid the kids that were running up and down, and the errant leg or elbow poking out from the seats next to him. It was then that he noticed the man standing by Lyndsey. He was broad, barrel-chested, and with a nose that was almost flat against his face. He looked like an old-time boxer, his dark hair cut short against his scalp and his hands covered in an assortment of platinum rings.

"Everything okay here?" he asked Lyndsey, as he waited for the man to step aside.

"Yes, fine," Lyndsey said, but her eyes betrayed her.

"It's Uncle Codey," A.J. added.

The man thrust out a hand. "Hi. Name's Codey Diedrich. We haven't met."

"No, we haven't," Matt replied, taking the man's hand. His grip was firm but his palm was slick.

"I was just saying hi to Lyndsey here, on account of us not having seen each other in a while."

"Right," Matt said. "I'm guessing you're related to her deceased husband?"

The man seemed to jerk at that. "Yeah. You could say that."

"Codey is Mason's brother," Lyndsey said, but her words sounded thin.

"Okay," Matt said, watching the guy's expression. "I'm sorry for your loss."

"Thank you."

Matt peered along the walkway. "Are you...traveling alone?"

"No, I'm with a couple of pals. Got some business in Philly we need to take care of, if you know what I mean."

Matt knew exactly what the guy meant, and he wondered whether the goon's chance encounter with his ex sister-in-law meant that their itinerary would suddenly get adjusted.

"Well, it was nice to meet you," Matt said, meaning to take his seat.

"Yeah, yeah. Lyndsey, stay in touch. Pa's been meaning to speak to you about some things. He was pretty shocked when you and A.J. took off."

"I'm not sure I want to do that," she said, speaking calmly and deliberately.

"Why's that?"

"You know why, Codey."

"Pa' was good to you."

"Oh really? Is that what you think?" She glanced at A.J. who was listening to every word. "Look, I really don't want to talk about this in front of Anna Jayne."

"Why not, Mom?" A.J. asked. "What's going on?"

"Grown up stuff," Lyndsey replied.

"I'm a grown up."

"I really think you oughtta reconsider, Lyndsey," Codey said. "For both of your sakes."

"Is that some kind of a threat, buddy?" Matt sniped.

"Just a fact."

"Then, I suggest you take your so-called facts back to your seat and leave the lady alone."

Codey squared up to him. "Who the hell did you say you were again?"

"The guy who's doing a much better job of taking care of these two than your shit stain of a brother ever could."

The passengers sitting around them suddenly took notice, and everything went silent. Matt watched the goon as his face shifted. He was obviously trying to figure out what his next move was. His hand clenched and unclenched, and the muscles in his jaw flexed as his eyes narrowed.

"Okay, big guy," Codey said after a moment. "You wanna make an enemy, that's fine by me. But when this thing hits the ground, we'll be waiting."

"I'll be looking forward to it," Matt said, shooting the guy a cock-eyed smile.

As the tension in the air built, and the two men glared at each other, Matt began to get the feeling that something was wrong. *Something definitely wasn't right.*

Codey made a gesture with his thumb and finger as if he were loading a gun, and grinned. "See you on the other side, Lyndsey."

He turned and walked away, and Matt stood there for a minute, watching as the big guy sat down and the two men sitting next to him glanced over their shoulders.

"Thank you," Lyndsey said as he dropped into the chair. "I didn't expect to see them."

"I get the feeling they meant to see you," he said. "I'm guessing they've been watching the airline booking system, and saw your name come up."

"Oh no," she said, waiting until A.J. placed her headphones onto her ears. "What are we going to do?"

"Don't worry. I'll take care of it."

"How?"

He shook his head. "Don't know, but I'll think of something."

She reached an arm across and hugged him then, nuzzling his neck. "I'm so glad I found you, you know that, Mr Groover? Why couldn't we have met years ago?"

"Life doesn't work like that, Lyndsey," he replied. "It just doesn't."

As he wrapped his hand around hers and closed his eyes, thankful that his life had taken such an unexpected and magical turn, the lights went out and the plane lurched forward.

That was when all hell broke loose.

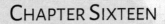

CHAPTER SIXTEEN

Collect the Bodies

The plane was filled with the terrified, blood-curdling screams of passengers fearing for their lives as the world rushed by outside, white plumes roaring past them at frightening speeds.

"What's going on?" Lyndsey yelled. "Matt, what's happening?"

"Mom?" A.J. cried. "Mom? Is this okay?"

The decompression masks dropped from overhead and Matt helped A.J. place hers over her mouth.

"It's okay," he said. "Just stay calm. I'm sure every-thing will go back to normal in a moment."

The air in the cabin was becoming increasingly thin, so he put his own mask on, peering at Lyndsey over the top. Her eyes were glistening with looming tears.

"Is this it?" she whispered to Matt. "Are we going to die?"

"Of course not," he said, gripping her hand, but he really didn't know. This was all his fears combined. He felt helpless, unable to influence the outcome in any way.

Heavy luggage came crashing down from the stor-age areas overhead, knocking one of the passengers out cold. People who had been innocently walking up and down the aisles prior to whatever the hell had just happened lay stranded on the ground, their legs trailing behind them. Matt wanted to help them, but he needed to stay with Lynsdey and A.J. He needed to ensure they were okay.

He watched as the ground rushed toward them, the plane barely holding any sort of trajectory. The flaps weren't operating at all, which meant the pilot had no control over anything. Matt knew if they hit the ground at the wrong angle, they were all dead. There was no getting away from that.

He was a soldier, military trained, but there was nothing in his training that could prepare anybody for this. For some reason, the plane had no electricity, which either meant the electronics had all failed at the same time, including all the triple redundant backups he knew commercial airliners had to have, or something sinister was at play. Either way, the earth was coming at them fast.

There was a screeching sound, as if the whole world was being wrenched from them, and the plane jerked as the wings seemed to stretch unnaturally.

"Brace!" one of the cabin crew yelled, his voice tremulous and shrill. "For God's sake, brace!"

Matt turned to Lyndsey and A.J. "Put your head between your legs!" he yelled. "I love you both. I just want you to know that! With everything I have!"

"Don't say that!" she screamed. "It sounds so final! This can't be it!"

She turned to him, tears rolling down her cheeks as the panic set in. She hugged A.J., who was sobbing beside her, and she gripped his hand so hard that her knuckles white. She went to speak, as if she'd remembered something important, something that had been eluding her, but then there was a crash as loud as anything Matt had ever experienced on the battlefield and everything went black.

He came to, blood trickling from a wound in his head, his vision swimming with black flashes. He was strapped to his seat with the remains of his mask pulled tight across his cheeks. Nothing remained of the cockpit up ahead. The front of the plane was dug into the earth, as if the aircraft had tried to burrow its way underground. The wings had disappeared too, like the wings of a butterfly, pulled away and discarded. There was a hole in the side of what remained of the cabin, blood dripping from torn metal.

He waited for his head to stop swimming and peered to his right. Where Lyndsey and A.J. had been sitting beside him, there was nothing. The chairs had been ripped away like pages from a book. He reached down to his seatbelt, but it was twisted and embedded in his hip. Blood oozed from the wound.

"Lyndsey!" he cried out. "A.J!"

He pulled at the clasp, smashing it with the palm of his hand as he cried out in pain, until it eventually came loose. He tugged his mask from his face and stood, but he immediately collapsed to his knees, as if everything that was holding him together had just evaporated.

"Lyndsey!" he cried once more. "Where are you?"

Behind him, a passenger lay embedded on what remained of his chair, the arm rest jutting from his chest as his head sagged, blood pooling on the floor. Behind him, an elderly woman lay with a suitcase jammed between her chest and head, her neck obviously broken.

Matt grabbed his stetson, and clambered over dead bodies and detritus, moving toward the hole in the cabin wall. Sunlight poured in from outside as survivors staggered in a zombie-like daze, looking for loved ones.

"Have you seen my Cindy?" one guy said. "She was just here. She doesn't like to be on her own."

A mother was pulling clothes from the ground, scurrying in the wreckage, searching for her son. "Teddy!" she cried. "Teddy. Where are you?"

Matt fell to the floor as he climbed from the aircraft. He couldn't believe what he was looking at. The airplane lay in pieces, like a toy that had been stepped on. The engines lay someway in the distance, bright orange flames leaping from the still spinning blades, black smoke trailing into the blue sky. Bodies lay scattered, many missing limbs, some completely decapitated.

He went from torso to torso, looking for Lyndsey and A.J., hoping to God he didn't find them.

He spied a woman on her haunches, peering into the distance. She had blond shoulder-length hair, and his heart leapt in his throat. He went to her, limping from the wound in his thigh. He had to see her. He had to make sure she was okay. He grabbed her arm, and turned her toward him.

"Lyndsey?" he said, but when the woman turned around, half her face had been caved in and her teeth were visible through her split cheek. She peered up at him through bloodshot blue eyes. *It wasn't her.*

"Help me," she said. "Please." But Matt moved away in horror, clambering across the torn Earth, falling over the wreckage, dragging himself away.

Matt fell to his knees, his body no longer able to hold his weight. *Why hadn't he listened to his instincts? Why hadn't he followed his gut and dragged them out of that airport? Why had this happened to them?*

His eyes moved to the remains of the forest, the trees ablaze. They were high up in the mountains, miles away from rescue. He had no idea what had happened, but he knew they needed help. He could see maybe 10 or 12 survivors, staggering around as if intoxicated. Some of them were terribly wounded and wouldn't make it through the night.

"What the hell's happening?" he said as he pulled himself to his feet. He reached into his pocket and retracted his phone, but no matter how often he pushed the power button, it remained inactive. *Dead*. He glanced at his watch, but the hands had stopped spinning completely.

"Wait a minute." He turned to another survivor, a woman in her 50s. "Do you have a phone?" he asked.

"What? I—"

"Do you have a phone? Hurry! This is important!"

She reached into her jacket, fumbled with her glasses, and found it. He snatched it from her.

"Hey!" she cried. "Just wait a minute!"

He held it up, jabbed at the power button, and tossed it back to her. "It's not working," he said. "Nothing is working."

He looked down at his wounded leg, pulling back at his torn pants. The wound was long and deep, blood streaming down his leg. His head wound was pretty bad too. He could feel the blood running down the back of his neck, soaking his shirt. The pain was bad, but nothing compared to how he was feeling. He felt sick to his stomach. He had to find Lyndsey, he had to find the kid. He had told them everything was going to be okay, and yet here he was, alone, standing among the dozens of bodies and mess, a passenger airline in bits on the ground, trees laying smashed, obliterated, burning.

He saw a body in the distance, lying in the undergrowth, face down and not moving. Familiarity leapt in his chest and he pushed the thought away.

"No," he said. "No, no, *no*."

He limped across the uneven ground, desperately trying to get to the body. It was a woman, blond hair, slim figure. She wasn't breathing. He stooped down and placed his hands on her shoulders. He smelled her scent, the perfume he had noticed the first day at the coffee shop. He knew instantly it was her.

"Lyndsey, *Lyndsey*?" He turned her over as gently as he could. Her eyes were open, staring at him, unseeing. She looked like she was sleeping but he knew she had gone, just as he knew the child's body a few feet away was A.J. He clenched his fists, wanting to strike something, anything. He'd just turned his life around, and now everything had been taken away from him—more importantly, the two people he cared about the most had had their lives erased, as easily as someone might throw away trash or turn off a lamp.

"I'm so sorry," he said, closing her eyes and placing his jacket over her face. "I'm so, so sorry."

There was a man's voice from somewhere behind him and he stood, recognizing the tone instantly. The guy with the barrel chest and short, dark hair was bloodied, a thick gash ripping his shirt in two, his upper body covered in blood.

"What...happened?" Codey Dietrich asked. "Is that...Lyndsey? A.J?"

Matt couldn't control the anger that was rising in his chest, and he launched himself for the man, swinging a right hook that connected with his jaw and sent him sprawling on the ground.

"You don't get to speak her name," he said. "You and your fucked up family put her and the kid through hell, and now look what's happened."

"You can't pin this on me," Codey replied, holding out his hands defensively. "You can't pin this on anyone."

"Don't tell me what I can and can't do!" Matt pulled him up by the collar and swung another fist, this time connecting with the guy's nose, sending a spray of blood down his lips and chest. "All she wanted was to be looked after, as a wife should, and yet your lowlife brother treated her like dirt, and you all stood around watching."

"No!" Codey cried. "It wasn't like that!"

Matt struck him again, driving him back to the ground, and he reached for a thick branch of dense wood, holding it high in the air, meaning to bring it down on the guy's skull.

"Wait!" another man cried. "Just wait."

Matt turned to see an older man approaching them. He had silver hair, parted at the middle, and small, dark eyes. He too was wounded, blood seeping from his nose and ear.

"Whatever you're doing here, friend," the old guy said, "it's not gonna bring them back."

"This here ain't any of your business, old timer," Matt replied.

"Maybe not, cowboy, but I don't like seeing a man throwing his life away when he's not thinking straight."

"I'm thinking just fine."

"Doesn't seem that way to me."

"Then you ain't seeing things the way I am."

The old guy held out a hand. "Name's Otto." Matt looked down at the wiry fingers and liver spotted skin, and declined to take it. "Suit yourself," Otto said. "Look, I was flying alone, so I can't say I know what you're going through, but I've got people in town that are waiting for me—people I want to see and I've got no way of getting to them. I'm going to need some help, and you, cowboy, look like the kind of guy who can assist me."

Matt glared at the old man, trying to figure out if he was being sincere. "She's dead," he said, pointing toward Lyndsey's body, "her daughter, too. They were all that I had."

Otto looked across at them and shook his head. "It's a damn shame, that's what it is. A downright tragedy. But beating up on that fella ain't gonna heal your grief, just like killing a man ain't gonna make things right."

Matt removed his stetson and ran a hand through his hair. He knew the old guy was right, but he had so much anger, so much rage. Everything he touched seemed to turn to shit, and he just didn't know how to stop it. He'd lost them, he really had. It was eating away at him, making him want to vomit.

"Can you help me?" Otto asked. "Can you help those of us who are still breathing?"

Matt didn't know how to answer that. He didn't think he was the right guy to help anyone. It seemed like those who came into contact with him either ended up leaving him or dying. One thing was for certain, his faith was being tested to the limit and the jury was out on which way it would turn.

"We need to collect the bodies," he said, his voice hoarse. "And I gotta deal with this jerk."

However, when he turned back to where he'd left Lyndsey's brother-in-law, he was gone.

CHAPTER SEVENTEEN

A Whole New Riddle

M att worked with the other survivors to collect the bodies together, trying to be as respectful as possible during what was a difficult task. Matt handled Lyndsey and A.J. himself, trying not to look at their lifeless faces as he covered them with blankets located in one of the aircraft's storage units. There were ten of them in all, including Otto, Codey Dietrich, and the lady with the phone, Geneva. Aside from a middle-aged guy called Sidney and a fat man named Gunn, the rest of the survivors were too injured to assist. The lady with the collapsed face was clinging on to life and another guy, who's leg was literally hanging by a thread, looked deathly pale.

With the work completed, Matt set about searching the remains of the plane for clothes to keep them warm and some food. He had to keep himself busy to blot out his grief. He couldn't think of A.J. lying there like a doll, her face waxy and still. He couldn't think of Lyndsey, her beautiful face like a mannequin, her eyes dark and soulless. He didn't know why they had been taken and not him. Surely it was his time.

He pulled open storage units, food trolleys, and overhead lockers, collecting everything he could and jamming it all into two suitcases that he'd found scattered around the aircraft. Ahead of him lay what remained of the tiny kitchen unit, and he headed for it, scrambling over twisted metal and shards of plastic. On its side lay the drinks trolley. The coffee pot was smashed on the floor and paper cups lay strewn across what was left of the aisle. However, inside were tiny bottles of liquid, the type of liquid that used to keep him company from the moment he rose in the morning until he went to bed.

He eyed the tiny bottles of vodka and whiskey, his mouth salivating at what lay inside. He could almost feel the acidic burn as the alcohol slipped down his gullet and entered his stomach. He could taste the cold, sharp liquor and could sense the buzz building behind his eyes, numbing his senses. *Just a little taste*, he thought. *One won't hurt.*

"Don't do it, cowboy," Otto said, standing behind him. "It ain't worth it."

"You following me around now?" Matt hissed, adjusting his hat.

"Just looking out for a friend."

"Are we friends now?"

"I like to think so," Otto replied, plucking the bottle of vodka from Matt's fingers. "I'm guessing the AA, 12-step program."

Matt nodded, wondering how the hell the old timer knew. "Four months dry," he said. "But can't help but think, if there was ever a time I was gonna fall off the wagon, this would be it."

"That's a long road, cowboy, and not one I'd recommend going down."

"Yeah, well," Matt scowled, grabbing the miniature bottle and unscrewing the top. "Your partner's not laying out there under a bedsheet, her daughter lying cold beside her. If I wanna have a drink, I'm damn well gonna have one."

There was the sound of a ruckus outside and Matt pushed past Otto, heading for the torn hole in the side of the United Airline B737's fuselage. Outside, the fat guy, Gunn, was sitting on his ass, blood pouring from his nose.

"What the hell's going on out here?" he bellowed.

"That guy punched me," Gunn said, pointing at Codey.

"Well, you shouldn't have got in my way, fat ass."

Matt stepped down from the plane and approached the pair. "Listen, we're up here in the mountains, miles away from civilization, with no way of contacting the emergency services. Our best bet is to sit tight and wait for help to come. It's going to be a long day, and the last thing we should be doing is fighting among ourselves."

"Says the man who suckerpunched me twice," Codey hissed. "And, in any case, this fatso tried to take my wallet."

Matt glared at the guy sitting on the ground. "Is that true?"

"That's not his wallet," he said, dabbing at the blood. "He was rummaging through the jackets, looking for anything he could take."

Matt glanced at both of them. "Wait. What jackets?"

Gunn slowly rose to his feet as the others circled them. He pointed at the dozens of bodies lying under scattered blankets. "Their jackets."

Codey backed away, holding up his hands. "Come on," he said. "I was just checking to see who these people are, that's all."

"Then why did you take that guy's money?" Gunn yelled. "And his credit cards?"

Geneva stood among them, her mouth open wide. "How could you do such a thing?"

"Hey, we don't know what's going on down in the towns. You saw what happened up there. The plane just cut out, as if everything just powered down, and none of our phones work anymore. What's that about? And when Sidney climbed up into that tree a little while ago, he said he saw columns of smoke rising from the valley. Ain't that right, Sid?"

The guy with the paunch and thick mustache shuffled his feet before nodding his head. "Yeah, I did. Something is definitely going on, and I got people down there."

"We all do," Otto interjected, "but that doesn't justify looting from the dead."

"Yeah, well, I'm just thinking ahead, that's all."

Matt shifted his hat and approached Codey, his hands balled into fists. "Your own men are lying dead over there, pal, and your niece. You wanna steal from them, too?"

"No, of course not. But, come on—"

"From this point on, I even catch you looking in their direction, you and I are gonna finish what we started a little earlier. You get me?"

The two men held each other's stare, neither willing to back down, before Codey flinched, a smile spreading across his lips. "Okay, okay. If that's what you want, I'll do as you say. But when the chips are down, you'll be surprised what you'll do."

The younger man walked away, leaving Matt to face Otto once more.

"A leader like you needs to keep his wits about him," the old guy said. "Especially if you're going to have to control characters like that. Can't be drinking yourself into a stupor."

"I'm not a leader," Matt replied. "Never wanted to be."

"And yet, here we are," Otto said. "If anyone's going to get us out of this, I say it's gonna be you."

"I agree," Geneva said, approaching them. "You got my vote, mister."

"And mine," Stanley added, followed by a "Hell yeah," from Gunn.

Matt stood in the center of them, wondering how the hell everything had spun out of control to the point where he was now the appointed leader of a group of airplane survivors, stranded in the mountains without any way of calling for help. It was like the sandbox once more, except this time, instead of masked insurgents and IEDs, they were facing a night in the wilderness with four of their number badly wounded and one who was about as trustworthy as Richard Nixon.

The problem was, he didn't feel like doing anything at all. He wanted Lyndsey, he wanted the one person he couldn't have. He wanted to lay down and hold her, feel her again, kiss her one last time.

"Well then, I suggest we hunker down," Matt said, "see what we can do to make the wounded as comfortable as possible, and hope to God help turns up soon."

That afternoon, the lady with her face caved in passed. Her name was Cecilia, Cee Cee for short. She'd been heading to Bedford with her husband to visit their daughter and grandchildren, but Bill had died in the crash and now she'd drifted away in her sleep. Whatever had happened was claiming so many lives and ruining so many more. One thing Codey had said had been right: The plane had simply shut down. It hadn't been a malfunction or a technical issue. The whole vehicle had simply stopped working. All the lights had gone out, there had been no communication from the flight deck, and there had been no attempt to pull up. They had been in a missile, barreling through the sky at over 500 miles an hour with no means of steering.

Geneva had some medical training, so she set to work on giving the three remaining wounded passengers as much medication and dressing as she could muster. There was the guy whose leg was literally hanging off called Chuck, a young girl with a broken arm named Jennifer, and a beanpole of a man with a fractured skull called Timothy. She wasn't a surgeon or a doctor, so she could only make matters superficially better, but it was all they had, and Matt was hoping she wouldn't have to hold the fort for long.

Codey skulked in the corner of the clearing made by the stricken plane, the flames now no more than smoldering embers. Matt didn't trust him and he certainly didn't like him, but they needed to use all the resources they had. One thing he learned in the military was to keep your enemies close, and he had no intention of letting the brother of Lyndsey's deceased husband out of his sight.

Sidney and Otto collected wood for a fire, and stacked it in the center of the clearing. Matt had built a tripod and hung a metal drawer from it that he'd found in the plane, and he'd filled it with chili beef that he'd located inside. If they were going to have to spend the night out in the open, they were going to eat. If help didn't come by sun-up, he planned to go find it himself. If he didn't, there was every chance more of them would die—particularly Chuck and Timothy, who looked about as gray as slate.

As the sun started to dip toward the horizon, Matt collected some more blankets from inside and handed them out. "Here," he said. "Everybody keep warm. It can get mighty cold up in the mountains when the sun disappears."

"Sounds like you know what you're talking about," Gunn replied, tucking the blanket beneath his chin.

"Did some training exercises in similar environments when I was in the military," Matt said. "They dropped us off in the middle of the night, miles from the base, and high up in the hills, and told us to find our way home. That first night, I got so cold, I thought they were gonna find me frozen in a block of ice."

Otto laughed. "Doesn't sound like appropriate training for the desert."

"You'd be surprised. It drops to below zero in the winter months. If you're out on maneuvers, sitting on top of a humvee with nothing but your ballistic vest and uniform to protect you from the elements, you feel it soon enough."

Sidney lit the fire, and they all watched as the flames slowly clambered up the mound of dry twigs and kindling. Before long, it was a roaring flame, throwing off enough heat to warm them. Codey moved closer and agreed to stir the chili, handing out generous servings in foil trays with plastic cutlery when it was done.

"This isn't bad," Jennifer said, her arm in a splint and strapped across her chest. "For airplane food, that is."

Matt grinned. "We're all still in shock, so getting anything in our stomachs is a bonus. Keeping it down will be a much bigger challenge."

They sat around the campfire, all speaking about those they'd lost, and their loved ones who were, very possibly, caught up in whatever the hell was going down.

"I lost my boyfriend," Jennifer said, tears glistening in her eyes. "He was in the men's room when the plane dropped. I didn't even see what happened to him."

"I was with my daughter," Sidney said, lighting a cigarette. "I saw her get thrown from the plane when we hit the dirt. She didn't stand a chance."

"My mom's expecting me," Chuck said, blood oozing from the dressing around his shattered leg. "She's cooking meatballs. She's going to be so mad."

"How about you, Matt?" Timothy asked, his voice groggy, his skull wrapped in a thick bandage. His eyes were glazed over, as if he were barely there.

Matt took a moment to compose himself, pulling his stetson over his eyes. "I was traveling with a woman I'd been seeing. Her daughter, too." He glanced at Codey who's own eyes remained fixed on the floor. "We were heading to see her mom. I think we stood a chance of building a life together, but all that's gone now."

"Who you got back home?"

"No one," he said without hesitation. "Don't have nothing. Just the church, and the reverend too, I guess."

"You don't look like the God-fearing sort," Codey said, a wry smile on his lips.

"I don't fear him," Matt answered. "Just put my faith in him."

"And how's that playing out for you?"

"Not sure yet. Maybe one day, all of this will make sense."

"How so?"

"I don't know. I just know that all the time I'm still breathing, I have to believe there's an answer."

Codey stood. "Well, you let me know when you've figured it all out. Right now, I gotta take a piss."

As the conversation subsided, and people started to drift into what Matt guessed would be fitful sleep, their nightmares filled with blood-curdling screams and the piercing sound of hard metal hitting rocks and soil, Otto leaned closer to him.

"What are you thinking?" he asked. "We obviously can't stay here another night."

Matt tossed a log onto the fire and eyed the hills. "Those of us who can walk, we head out in the morning. Go find help."

The flames flickered in Otto's eyes like flitting, yellow fingers as he wiped his hand across a day's worth of white stubble. "And if there's no help to find?"

"Then we got a whole new riddle to solve, old man. A whole new problem."

CHAPTER EIGHTEEN

The Gathering Storm

M att lay in the darkness, his stetson over his eyes, listening to the howl of the coyote and the scurrying of tiny animals in the undergrowth. The wound in his leg was throbbing, and his head was pounding. His body felt like it had been beaten into submission by a thousand pummeling fists, but much worse than that, his mind was all over the place.

The first time he'd seen her, he'd known. Like 300-volts spiking through his torso, he had been sparked into action. Her eyes, her hair, the way she looked at him, as if she'd known him all her life. That moment kept playing over and over, backward and forward, a silent movie repeating and repeating until he couldn't take it anymore. They had meant to have a life together, but they'd had no more than a few weeks.

He sat up, certain that something was rummaging around the fire. He peered into the darkness, wondering if there were wolves roaming the mountains. He searched around him for a branch or a rock, meaning to chase whatever it was away, and that was when he saw her. She was sitting up, and the blanket had slipped around her waist. Her face was gaunt and gray, but her beauty shone through.

"Lyndsey?" he said. "You shouldn't be moving. You were badly hurt."

She pulled the blanket away and stood, just as A .J. started to stir beside her. Aside from their pallid complexions, they looked just the way they had when they'd boarded the plane. They moved toward the remains of the campfire, the dying embers illuminating their features, making them seem ghostlike, almost spiritual.

He went to them, feeling as though there was hope, as if the life he had thought he was racing toward had somehow been reborn. It didn't make any logical sense, but he didn't care.

"Are you okay?" he whispered, eyeing the sleeping bodies scattered around him. "I thought you were gone. I should have been more thorough when I checked. I'm so sorry."

"You did this," Lyndsey said. "This is your fault."

Her words were like shards of glass, cutting him to the bone. "What do you—"

"The people you killed," A.J. added. "The people you hurt. Your unborn child."

Matt shook his head. "No, I didn't mean for that to happen, for any of it to happen."

"This was payback," Lyndsey said. "For everything you've ever done."

"You will never be happy," A.J. said. "You'll never be free."

They turned and walked away, disappearing into the gloom, and Matt fell to his knees, shaking his head. "It wasn't my fault," he said. "It wasn't my fault."

Everything was so screwed, so twisted. The way that they had been taken from him, the way the man he had thought to be his father had killed both his mothers, how Kenzo and then Chris had been obliterated by the war. One thing he knew for certain: Life had a way of kicking you in the face when you were sitting in the park and looking up at the sunshine. He wasn't about to let it happen again. If he had to step on a few toes, break a few bones to protect himself, then that's what he was going to do. He'd had enough of being the fall guy. From now on, he looked out for number one, and everybody else could go to hell.

The sunlight brought him back to reality with a bang. He sat up and blinked. He was laying so close to the embers that ash was on his hands and in his hair.

"Whoa," Codey said. "You get a little cold in the night there, cowboy?"

Matt turned his head and studied the wounded. Chuck wasn't moving, and his eyes were open, staring at some unseen spot high above him. He checked his pulse, which was non-existent. His skin was cold, his body gradually stiffening.

"Sorry, Chuck," he said, pulling the blanket over his face. "We can't stay here any longer, people. It's clear that help isn't on the way, so we're going to have to help ourselves."

Gunn emerged from the trees, zipping his pants. "You sure that's a wise move? I mean, what if we head out, and then the emergency services arrive."

"If that was gonna happen, it would have happened already," Otto chipped in. "These planes have black boxes that are tracked. If they were gonna come, the helicopters would have arrived a couple of hours after we crashed."

"But, what about—" Gunn glanced at the scores of bodies, laying motionless. He whispered, "What about the dead?"

"We bury them here," Matt replied, his voice cold and emotionless. "We dig a grave for every single one, and I'll give the blessings."

"But, what about their families?" Geneva asked. "They should be here when they...you know?"

"When we find a town and figure out what the heck is going on, we'll send a party up here to exhume them." Matt grabbed his jacket. "But, in the meantime, we have to focus on survival. I'm still alive, and I plan on staying that way."

The dig and the internements took a few hours. The ground was harder than Matt would have liked, and they used shards of metal from the wreckage—pieces of chairs and the internal structure—to scrape at the Earth. It wasn't ideal, but they used what they had.

When it came to burying Lyndsey and A.J. he went to a place within himself—the place he'd discovered in Iraq. It was a cold spot, stark and damp. Very little light penetrated, and there was no love there, no emotion. It was the place he visited when he had to pull the trigger, unloading another volley from the .50 cal, cutting other humans in half as if they were made from sand. They lowered the bodies into the ground, the smaller body beside her mother, and Matt said a prayer.

"Oh Lord, we humbly entrust Lyndsey and Anna Jayne to you. In this life, you embraced them with your tender love. Deliver them now from every evil and bid them eternal rest. The old order has passed away; welcome them into paradise, where there will be no sorrow, weeping, or pain, but fullness of peace and joy with your Son, Jesus Christ and the Holy Spirit." He paused, desperately trying to stay within that damp, cold, emotionless hole, but feeling emotion welling within him, rising in his chest, threatening to explode.

Otto grabbed him by the shoulder, and finished for him. "Forever and ever. Amen."

Matt fell to his knees, gripping the soil and tossing a handful into the makeshift grave. "I'm gonna miss you both," he said, his voice cracking with emotion. "I don't think I ever told you I loved you, but I did. *I do.* I wish it was me in there, not you. You didn't deserve this. You were right, this is my punishment—this is my penance."

Codey approached the grave and tossed a handful of soil into the hole. "See ya, Lyndsey and A.J. I'm sorry how it all turned out, but you have to know, we cared for you. We all did."

Matt glanced at the guy, trying hard not to leap up, grab him by the throat, and tear his head from his shoulders.

"You okay down there, cowboy?" Otto said, standing beside him. "You know, you don't need to rush. Take as long as you need."

Matt wiped the remnants of a tear from his eye and stood. "What I need is to get the hell away from this place."

"You sure about that?"

Matt grabbed a makeshift shovel and started piling the dirt into the hole. "Never been more sure of anything my entire life."

They walked down the hillside, snaking through the forest, avoiding any treacherous descents and areas of densely packed woodland. Matt knew there were bears in the hills, and he was constantly on the lookout for dung and signs of dens.

Their speed was hampered by the wounded. Jennifer cried out in pain whenever her broken arm made contact with a branch or a bush, and Timothy was still suffering from the remnants of concussion, making it difficult for him to traverse the rough terrain. Gunn was slow, too. He clearly wasn't used to walking, and was certainly no mountain hiker.

Matt thought of what he'd left behind, of the bodies in the ground, but he fought to push the thoughts away. He had one goal now, and that was to find help. If he could do that and figure out what had happened, he could then turn his attention to recovering Lyndsey and A.J. and giving them a proper burial in a place he could visit. He owed them that much.

"You sure we're heading in the right direction?" Codey asked. "Sure feels like we're moving in circles."

"I'm sure."

"Because I'm pretty certain we saw that fallen pine about an hour ago."

"Lot's of fallen pines in these woods."

"Yeah, but—"

"Look, pal," Matt hissed. "You want to cut your own trail, go ahead. Nobody's keeping you here."

Codey held up his hands. "No, I'm not saying that. It's just—"

"It's just, what? Look, I was in the military in Iraq? Were you there?" Codey's gaze shifted, and he shook his head. "I didn't think so. First thing they teach you in training is how to navigate through rough terrain, and you see that great big, shining ball of light in the sky?" Codey looked up. "That's the best navigation tool there is, and right now, it's taking us toward civilization."

With the dispute settled, Matt pushed them on. He knew the towns of St. Marys and Bedford were some way in the distance, maybe 50 miles or more, but they had no time to waste. Their provisions were meager at best, and while they'd been lucky with the weather so far, he also knew that when the clouds rolled in, they would be soaked to the skin in no time at all. They had to find shelter before nightfall, and that meant they had to keep moving.

After a couple of hours of intense walking, there was the sound of earth slipping behind him, followed by a clatter and a woman's piercing scream. He turned to see Jennifer sprawled on the ground, her arm bent at an unnatural angle.

"Holy shitting Christ!" she yelled, clenching her teeth.

"What happened?" Geneva asked, rushing to her.

"Slipped on the dirt," Jennifer said, holding her arm. "We're going too fast. You're making us go too fast!" she cried, glaring at Matt.

"You want to get outta here or what?" he hissed back.

"Maybe we should take a break," Sidney said. "We've been going for hours."

"Yeah," Gunn added. "My feet are killing me."

Timothy slid with his back to a tree, dropping to his knees. "I don't feel so good."

"Maybe they're right," Otto said, whispering into Matt's ear. "Maybe we do need to have a time out. Just for a little while."

Matt peered into the distance. Sure enough, there was a storm cloud building—and a big one, too.

"That hits us," he said. "And these people are going to be even more miserable than they are right now."

"Then, put it to the vote," Otto suggested. "Let the people decide. If you don't, you may find you have a mutiny on your hands."

He groaned, wishing he was on his own, making his own decisions. He'd promised himself that he was going to look out for number one—number one alone—and yet here he was, bending to every whine and complaint from a group of people he didn't even know. He didn't want to be a leader, didn't want to be the hero, and yet he found himself doing exactly what he'd sworn he wouldn't.

"Okay, people. Listen up. Over there is a storm cloud that looks about as angry as a bull in a bull pit. What's more, it's heading our way. We can either camp out here and hope the wind changes direction, or we can push on and look for shelter. I know what I would do, but Otto suggested we have a democratic vote, so that's what we're gonna do."

"Sounds like a good idea," Geneva said, re-attaching Jennifer's splint.

"I'm all for that," Gunn said, staring at a blister on his foot the size of a cherry.

"All those who want to find shelter, raise your hands." Otto's hand went up, as did Matt's own. "Okay. And, all those who want to camp out right here, raise your hands."

The air was filled with arms, fingers pointing to the heavens.

He turned and glared at his new friend.

"Well, you know what they say," the old guy said. Matt shrugged. Otto grinned. "If you don't wanna get wet, don't jump in the pool."

CHAPTER NINETEEN

Hot Coffee

And get wet, they did. The storm took about 30 minutes to make it across the valley, and in that time, the clouds became a dense, gray blanket that completely covered the sky overhead. Raindrops the size of snowballs poured from the heavens, penetrating the canopy and covering the ground around them, creating a river of mud and dirty water that raced down the incline. Their clothes were drenched in seconds and their hair became slick and stuck to their faces.

"This is no good," Matt cried. "We have to move."

"But the ground!" Codey yelled. "We'll break our necks if we try to go now."

"We sit in this for much longer, we'll be dead of hypothermia before we know what's hit us."

Matt spied a plateau some way in the distance, a hard patch of Earth with a rock face at its rear. He thought there was every chance that there would be an indentation in that rock, a place they could hide out in and wait for the rainfall to ease.

"This way!" he yelled. "Come on!"

Lightning streaked across the sky overhead, followed by a loud clap of thunder that shook the Earth all around them. The earth was giving way beneath them, the running water pushing soil further down the slope. Matt could feel the cold liquid penetrating his skin, soaking him through to the bones. They weren't dressed for hiking down a mountain. Every single one of them had come prepared to depart the airplane, get in a car or taxi, and head to a town. Suburban clothes were not suited to the great outdoors. Matt silently wished for his army fatigues and a tent. *What he would give for a tent.*

Gunn was lagging, and so Matt went to him, pulling him along. "Come on!" he yelled.

"I can't. My feet, they're hurting."

"They'll be hurting a whole lot more if we don't find shelter."

He wished he'd gone with his gut and pushed the group harder, made them walk another mile or two in search of a safer spot.

They reached the plateau as the trees thinned out, and now they were completely exposed to the elements. Matt peered over the edge at the drop that fell away beneath them.

"Be careful!" he shouted over the noise of the falling rain and the deafening thunder. "It's a long way down."

Sure enough, as soon as Timothy stepped onto the ledge, his right leg went out from under him and he slipped, almost toppling. Geneva grabbed his hand and pulled him back.

"Thank you," he said. "That was close."

"Yeah, too close," Geneva replied.

Matt saw an opening up ahead and he raced toward it. Another streak of lightning fizzed overhead, followed by another clap of thunder as the rainfall intensified. Mud fell from the rockface, splattering the hard earth beneath their feet, creating a squelching, soup-like texture that was treacherous underfoot. Matt glanced behind him and watched as the others gingerly maneuvered across the ledge. They were some 30 feet back.

"I think I've found something!" he yelled, approaching a semi-circular hole in the rocks, big enough to crawl through. He stooped down and peered inside, trying to make out the depth of the cave.

"Is it safe?" Otto asked, stooping beside him, his white hair stuck to his head, his scalp visible beneath the thin strands.

"Only one way to find out." Matt dragged himself through the hole, his knees deep in thick puddles. His hand clawed at loose stones and wet soil, and the rock above him scraped at his shirt and skin. The wound in his hip screamed out in agony as it clattered into the limestone, but he pushed onward, scampering through the black. The narrow tunnel bent round to his right and, beyond, it appeared to open up into a tall cavern that stretched into the mountainside.

There was a sharp light up ahead and Matt stood, heading for it. It was a yellow flare, like a tiny campfire. As he neared, he saw features resembling a man's face, followed by another younger person. He reached for his gun, but remembered he didn't have it. It was back home in Tennessee. He was unarmed and facing a threat he didn't understand. Maybe he'd just made the most stupid mistake of his life.

"Hello, friend," one of the men said. "Welcome to Coyote Hole."

The guy's name, as it turned out, was Hank, and the other guy standing beside him was his son, Tucker. They'd been out hunting when the storm had approached and, like the rest of them, their phones no longer worked.

They all stood in the cavern, listening as the rain pounded the earth outside, and the storm circled their position like a pack of baying wolves.

Matt told the pair about the flight they'd taken, the crash, and the scores of people that had died. The mood turned somber as each of them told stories of their loss, their emotions burning and raw. There were tears and hugs. It seemed to Matt like the storm had drawn the pain out, like poultice on poison, extracting it from the deepest, hardest parts of the human psyche, spilling it out of them like toxins.

Matt explained how the airplane had seemed to shut down, just like their phones. One minute it was cruising along, stable and smooth, and the next, it was hurtling headlong toward the Earth.

The story seemed to shake their new friends. "Now you mention it," Hank said. "Our flashlights weren't working either, or the walkie talkies we always bring along with us in case we get split up."

Matt groaned, as a grim realization set in. It was as if anything that was powered by electricity had simply ceased to be effective. If that was true, they were in a far worse predicament than he'd first thought. The whole world ran on juice, everything: homes, the internet, the financial system, even the goddamn government.

"What about mom?" Tucker asked. "Do you think she's okay?"

"I'm sure she's fine, son," Hank replied, trying to reassure him. "Once the storm has blown over, we'll head home. She'll probably be cooking dinner or chatting with the neighbors."

Matt looked away, trying to hide his expression. He sensed the storm was going to last a lot longer than these people realized, and it wasn't the rain he was worried about.

"How far's your home?" Matt asked.

"Oh, about six or seven miles. You're all welcome to join us. We can sit with you while you wait for the emergency services to arrive."

"That would be great," Gunn said, nursing his swollen feet. "I sure could use a shower, too, if you're offering."

"Of course," Hank replied. "All of you. Whatever you need."

"Let's not get ahead of ourselves," Matt said, trying to display some realism.

"What do you mean?" Jennifer asked, cradling her arm.

"Just that we don't know what to expect. Something strange is going on here, and we need to be prepared for the worst."

"Way to go, Groover," Codey sniped. "If the rain hadn't dampened the mood enough, you've just put the final nail in the coffin."

"What our friend means," Otto offered, "is that something has taken down all our communications, all our means of contacting the outside world, and it also took down our airplane. Until we know what it is, we should keep our minds open to any possibility."

Matt approached the cave mouth and looked outside as the rain began to ease. Behind him the group continued their animated debate. Some, such as Codey, were adamant that the world out there was carrying on as normal and what they had faced was some strange technical mishap that had only affected the peak of the mountain. Others however, Timothy included, were less optimistic. It turned out that the tall, thin guy was an astrophysicist, and worked in the Nuclear Physics Laboratory in Pittsburgh.

"Could be a flare," he said. "Solar. That could do this type of thing. Maybe. It would have to be extremely powerful, of course, to take down an aircraft, but it's possible—with the right circumstances, the right set of events."

"No way!" Gunn cried. "I've read about stuff like that. Superman used a super solar flare in comic book #38 to defeat Ulysses. Man, something like that could take down the whole world. Like, serious "end of days" stuff, you know what I mean?"

"This isn't a comic book, Gunn," Codey said. "Things like that don't happen in real life."

"Timothy?" Matt asked. "Could it?"

"All I say is, it's possible."

"Holy cow" Geneva exclaimed. "I had no idea."

"Oh yeah," Codey sniped. "You're trying to tell me some fireball from millions of miles away just magically blasted our plane out of the sky and took out our comms?"

"Not a fireball, dumbass," Jennifer said. "A flare. It's like a giant burst of energy."

Timothy nodded. "That's the gist of it."

"Sounds terrifying," Sidney added. "Something like that, you have to wonder what else it could have taken out."

"Depends on how powerful it really was," Timothy replied. "And that's assuming it was even that at all."

"The rain's stopped," Matt interjected. He was growing tired of the constant back and forth, and the nonsensical theorizing. They'd find out what had happened soon enough, but right now, survival was their number one priority. "If we're gonna make a push for Hank's home, I say we do it right now."

"Hell yeah!" Codey cried. "Hot coffee, here we come."

CHAPTER TWENTY

Free State

Matt saw it first. It was pretty innocuous, like a smear on the backdrop, hardly anything to be concerned about, but there it was, nevertheless. He adjusted his stetson and peered into the distance. He could see what looked like a road, winding through the mountain, snaking down the incline, but further down the valley—where he guessed Hank's hometown would be—there were a half dozen columns of smoke, rising into the air like tendrils. There was a scent on the breeze too, like burnt rubber.

He waited for signs of movement on the road, for a vehicle or a hiker, but there were none. It was as if the landscape was devoid of life, as if everything and everyone had departed in a hurry.

"That rifle loaded?" he asked Hank, pointing at his Ruger.

"Sure is. I was planning on getting me some deer today."

"It might not be deer you find yourself aiming at," Matt said to himself, turning away.

They continued their descent, but Matt's senses were on high alert. He didn't much care for the pillars of smoke or the deathly, unnatural silence. They were a group of unarmed civilians, some of them wounded, all of them tired. What they needed was a safe haven, not an uncertain, unpredictable outcome.

"Listen up," he said, turning to the others. "I reckon maybe Hank, Otto, and I should go and check out what's up ahead before y'all go any further."

Codey's eyes narrowed. "Why? What are you hiding from us?"

"Nothing. I just don't want to drag y'all down this hill for nothing."

"There's houses down there, ain't there?" Codey shot back. "People too. I don't want to spend any longer up this mountain than I absolutely have to."

"He's right," Hank added. "I wanna get home as soon as I can, and I know that my son wants that, too."

"Yeah," Tucker nodded. "I wanna see Mom."

Matt eyed Otto, who he'd noticed had also spied the smoke. They shared a knowing glance. "Matt's right," Otto said. "No point wasting energy until we know the way is clear. We've come too far to make any mistakes now."

"You're talking as though we've got something to fear," Codey said. "As if there's danger down there. Do you know something we don't, Groover?"

"You heard Timothy," Matt said. "Who knows what's going on?"

The group fell silent, their nervous glances followed by anxious shuffling.

"Oh, come on!" Codey cried. "You gotta be kidding me!"

"Maybe he's right," Gunn said. "This way might be safer."

Codey shook his head and spat. "Well, if you wanna stay up here and wait for another storm, do what the hell you want." He approached Matt, his lips pursed. "But I'm going with these guys."

The four of them moved swiftly along the trail, all the while Matt watched as the smoke up ahead grew in intensity and the scent became stronger. There was a crackling, spitting noise, too, and the occasional sound of a car horn.

"I don't like this," Otto whispered into his ear. "Don't like this at all."

They clambered onto the asphalt and followed the road that hugged the base of the mountain. No cars passed them, no trucks. It was as if the route had been closed, as though the road had been blocked somehow.

"Odd," Hank said. "This time of day, this road's usually bustling with traffic. I usually avoid it until rush hour has passed."

They rounded the bend, and before them lay dozens of vehicles, all lying motionless, scattered like kids' toys. There was a group of kids who Matt didn't like the look of moving among them.

"What the hell?" Codey cried. "Has there been an accident or something?"

Matt approached one of the youths—a teenage boy wearing a Phillies baseball cap. He had his head inside a Toyota RAV4 and was fishing around in the glove box.

"What you up to there, kid?" Matt asked, pulling his stetson down to shield his eyes from the glare of the emerging sun.

"None of your business," the kid growled.

"Hey, I'm just asking," Matt replied curtly. "Why are all these vehicles just sitting here, unoccupied?"

The kid turned to face him. "Beats me. Don't care. All I know is, all this stuff's just lying here unattended, and if we don't take it, somebody else will."

He grabbed a bag from the backseat, rifled through a purse, and helped himself to a handful of 20-dollar bills and a collection of credit cards.

"Police won't look too kindly on you looting, kid. You know that, right?" Matt said, watching as the boy moved to the next vehicle.

"Police ain't nowhere to be seen, man," he said, grinning. "Ain't coming, either. This here's what you call a free state, my man. And, guess what? Everything is just that. *Free*."

Codey opened the door of a dark blue Silverado and helped himself to a SIGP320 handgun from underneath the passenger seat.

"Hey," Philly-Cap yelled as he came sprinting from the next car over. "That's mine."

Codey smashed the butt of the pistol into the kid's nose, spraying blood all over the windshield. The boy crumpled in a heap. "Like you said kid, it's a free state."

"I don't get it," Hank said. "Why are none of these vehicles operable?"

Matt recalled what Timothy had said about the solar flair, but nothing about the deserted road made any sense. *Why had everybody run, leaving so many possessions behind?* It was like there had been some kind of panic.

Up ahead, the road ran through a small town that sat either side of the road. It was the kind of place that personified small town America, with its rustic looking buildings, a few local shops, and a decrepit looking church. Smoke billowed from somewhere a few blocks over.

"You want to check it out?" Otto asked. "Could be dangerous."

Matt paused to consider the question. "Well, we need to know what's going on."

"And I need to know if my wife's okay," Hank said, striding ahead.

They wound their way through the idle traffic, passing an eerily silent gas station and a burger joint with its windows smashed in. A homeless guy sat on the corner, eating food from a dumpster, the remains of cold, ketchup drenched fries hanging from his lips.

"It's the end of the world!" he yelled, fishing inside a paper bag for the remains of a grease soaked hamburger. "Get your kicks now, my friends, 'cause tomorrow might never come!"

A block ahead, a group of men were kicking in the front door to what looked to be a hardware store.

One of the guys reached in, retrieved a sledge hammer, and swung it at the window, sending shards of glass spraying in all directions. There were high-fives and a loud roar as the men entered, but not before the owner came out shooting. One of the men staggered backward with a hole in his chest the size of a grapefruit. Blood sprayed from his open mouth as he fell to his knees, and then his head exploded as another spray of buckshot demolished his skull.

The others retaliated by pulling the shopkeeper out by his hair as the gun tumbled from his grasp. He reached for it in desperation, crying out in agony as the men took turns to kick, punch, and stomp on him. His body convulsed and spasmed as each blow hammered into his flesh, cracking his bones and pulverizing his internal organs. Before long, he lay in a bloodied heap, his lifeless eyes staring as if pleading for help that was never going to come.

"What the hell?" Hank said, turning toward Matt. "What in the name of God is going on here?"

"I say we head back, regroup, and figure out our next move," Matt said, "before we get ourselves all mixed up in this mess." The whole scene was messing with his head. It reminded him of wandering the streets of Baghdad, watching as AQI members dragged men suspected of colluding with the allied forces from their beds, only to execute them right there in the street. He had watched too many husbands, sons, and brothers die.

"Not without my wife," Hank replied, his mouth drawn down in a terrified scowl. "Not without my Rosie."

Codey was the first to react. "Maybe we can ally ourselves with these guys, convince them to cut us in on whatever it is that they're up to."

"What?" Otto replied. "Did you not just see what happened? They just killed that man."

"He killed one of theirs first."

"Because they invaded his home."

"Right!" Codey exclaimed, his eyes bright and alive. "And now they have what he had. Look, you heard the kid back there. The police ain't coming. That's what he said. Whatever happened, whatever took down our plane, it's obviously got the authorities so distracted that they're unable to control the streets. I say, we get in on it before we're left behind—before we end up like that shopkeeper, bleeding out on the street while the rest of humanity does whatever it needs to do to survive."

"You're sick," Otto said. "If you think I'm going to behave like those animals, then think again."

"Then, maybe, it'll be you next."

Otto bared his teeth. "Say that again, you greasy, overweight, stinking pile of—"

"Okay!" Matt said. "Let's keep it together here. I say we don't make any rash decisions before we figure out what's happening. In the meantime, Hank has a wife to rescue and we're gonna help him do it. We owe him that much."

The warring pair glared at each other for a few more moments, before Otto backed away. "Yeah, I agree," he said, brushing his shirt down.

Hank let out a long breath before checking his rifle. "Then, let's go."

Hank's house sat in a quiet neighborhood. It was set back from the road with a large lawn separating it from the neighboring properties. As they passed the other houses, Matt saw drapes twitching and blinds being half-opened. A couple of times, he saw pairs of eyes peering into the streets, the hint of a rifle muzzle resting against the glass.

Up ahead, smoke billowed from a property, the front porch now just a smoldering pile of scorched timber.

"That's the Harper place," Hank said. "I hope they're okay."

"Let's get to your wife first," Matt replied. "We can come back for them once she's safe."

The door to the house across the street hung from its hinges, the front window cracked. The silence from inside was deafening. Matt peered into the opening, but the house was empty. The TV lay on the ground, its screen cracked, the floor littered with shattered china and splintered picture frames. The rear screen door was open, a bloody handprint on the wall. Matt ushered Hank away, not wanting him to see inside.

"This is bad," he said to Otto. "Looks like people are turning on each other, which usually means one thing."

"That people are desperate," Otto offered. "Or afraid. I don't know which one's worse."

"I'm guessing it's a bit of both."

Behind them there was the sound of gunfire as three white males ran from another property. The homeowner appeared in the doorway, a pistol in his hand. A bullet struck one of the fleeing burglars, but he kept running, glancing over his shoulder and giving his attacker the bird.

"Rosie!" Hank cried as they neared his home. There were bullet holes in the porch and window, and the car on the driveway had been damaged beyond repair. He climbed the porch steps two at a time and slammed his hand repeatedly on the door. "Rosie! It's me. Hank. I'm home. Let me in, baby."

There was no answer. Matt looked at Otto who shook his head. Codey walked toward the rear of the property, the Sig tucked in the waistband of his pants.

"Rosie! It's me. Come on. Let me in, honey. I don't know what's happening, but we need to get away from here." Still there was no answer. "I'm kicking it in," Hank said to Matt. "Will you help me?"

Hank kicked the door to no avail, so Matt slammed his shoulder into it. The first time it didn't give at all, but by the third, the frame gave way and they were inside. Hank rushed into the living room and then upstairs, his heavy boots pounding the carpet. Matt could hear him sprinting from room to room, opening and closing the doors.

"Rosie?! Baby! I'm home!"

Matt looked up, saw Codey standing in the kitchen, and realized the back door must have been unlocked. He was smirking and holding a slip of paper in his hand.

"Looks like she left a note," he said.

Hank descended the stairs, ran into the kitchen, and tore it from Codey's grasp. "Give that to me!" He held it up to the light as his eyes narrowed. "*Gone to get some groceries. Be back soon. Love, Rosie.* Oh, thank God." He bowed his head and fought back the tears. "I thought she was dead."

"Don't worry," Matt said. "If she's out there, we'll find her."

There was a rap at the door, and Matt whirled round, his fists clenched. It was the guy who had shot one of the burglars. He was tall, maybe six-foot-two, hispanic, with dark hair and glasses.

"Hey, Hank," he said. "Thought you were out hunting."

Hank went to him. "Roberto, have you seen my Rosie?"

"Not since yesterday," he replied, shaking his head. "She headed out, right before everything went to hell."

Hank's shoulders slumped. "What do you mean, went to hell? What's going on?"

"We don't know," Roberto replied. "Nobody's saying anything. All I know is, we got no power, no water, no telephones, no car. It just happened yesterday. Everything just shut down, all at once, as if somebody had pulled a lever and put the whole world on standby mode."

Matt couldn't believe what he was hearing. Without power and water, people were going to die. It was a recipe for anarchy, for militias, for violence.

"They came to my house, trying to steal our food. Luckily, I have a couple of weapons of my own and I managed to fight them off."

"We saw you hit one as he ran away," Codey replied. "Good shooting, buddy."

"Not good enough," Roberto replied. "I was aiming for his head."

"I need to find her," Hank said. "She's out there on her own. She's not good in a crisis. She needs me."

"We'll help you find her," Matt replied. "But if we don't get back to the others soon, they'll think something's happened and they'll come looking. They could walk straight into danger."

Hank's face turned ashen. "Oh, God. Tucker."

"Right," Matt said. "We need to make sure he's safe. The others too."

Matt could see Hank was torn. He didn't want to abandon his wife, but on the other hand, he had a son who needed him. He couldn't be in two places at once.

Otto interjected. "Might I make a suggestion?"

"I'm all ears," Hank said, trying to compose himself.

"We split our resources. Two of us head back to the others, fill them in on the details, and then bring them to the house. In the meantime, Hank, you stay here and see if you can find your wife."

Relief flooded across Hank's expression like a sunrise. "I like that," he said. "But you'll bring Tucker here as soon as you can?"

"Of course."

"I volunteer to stay here," Codey said, fingering the Sig. "I'll help Hank find his wife, and then maybe we can take a few potshots at the kids who tried to loot Roberto's family home."

Matt let out a long breath. He didn't trust Codey. The guy was a thug and a crook, but he knew the cards had been dealt and he had to play what he had.

"Okay, but don't go killing anybody."

"Hey," Codey replied. "I won't go looking for it, but if they shoot first..."

CHAPTER TWENTY-ONE

Ghost Town

They arrived back at camp a little after sunset. The walk back had been a quiet one, both men reeling from everything they had learned. If the town had been a microcosm of what was going on all around the country, Matt thought they were in big trouble.

He didn't know if what had happened had been caused by a solar flare, or some sort of cyber attack; but whatever it was, it had dealt at least the surrounding area a crippling blow. He thought back to everything that had happened to him, the pain he had suffered, and realized he needed to channel that emotion, that energy. He had been pounded and beaten, and yet he was still standing. He knew that if he was going to survive this latest disaster, he was going to have to make some decisions, and he suspected at least some of them would be unpopular.

"You're back," Geneva said, watching from the ridge as they climbed the slope. "But, wait a minute. Where are the others?"

"Let's get back to the camp and we'll fill you in."

Back at base, Matt recounted the events of the past few hours, with Otto adding his own perspective. As he spoke, the mood darkened. Tucker, in particular, was visibly shaken.

"So, my mom wasn't home?" he asked.

"No, kid, but your dad's stayed back. He and Codey are going to keep looking for her."

"But, what if she's injured—or worse?"

"We just have to hope that she managed to find someplace safe, or some friendly faces. I'm sure she did."

"And you say these people were shooting at each other?" Sidney asked, putting out a Chesterfield. "Why?"

Matt thought about that for a moment. "In my experience, when times get hard, people do irrational things. I saw that in Baghdad. People were being threatened, their families murdered, tortured until they couldn't take it anymore. I saw ordinary, civilized human beings becoming informants for the IQA in order to protect those they loved. When people are desperate, they become unpredictable."

"So, everybody's a threat." Gunn said. "Is that what you're saying?"

"Not everybody," Matt replied. "But we need to be cautious." He glanced at Tucker. "We have your rifle if we need to use it, and we know what we're facing. I say we head back to Hank's tomorrow, and once we're there, we figure out what to do next. Maybe, by then, the army will have arrived and things can start to get back to normal."

He thought of Lyndsey and A.J., and knew deep down that life would never be normal again. He also thought of his unborn son, and hoped that whatever was happening had not affected Tiffany and her new life. He couldn't bear to lose two kids in a matter of days.

"But I can't make you come," he added. "If you want to stay up here and wait it out, then that's entirely your choice."

He watched as each of them thought their options over. He knew it was a tricky decision. They were all now fully briefed on what was going on in the town, but they also knew that up there, in the hills, they were open to the elements as well as anyone else who came snooping around.

"You're the soldier," Jennifer said after a moment, wincing as she shifted her splint. "So, I say, we go with you."

The next day, Matt woke up early. He hadn't slept a wink. He kept thinking of the shopkeeper, the way those men had wiped him from the face of the Earth without even a hint of remorse. Then, he thought of Roberto chasing the burglars from his home, shooting one of them in the shoulder. Worst of all, he thought of Chris with a bullet in his head, his blood and brains all over the walls.

They slowly made their way toward the town, but this time, when they arrived at the road, it was no longer deserted. There were around a dozen people heading out of town, carrying backpacks, pushing trolleys full of their belongings, some of them carrying weapons. When Matt and the others emerged, the man in front swung his rifle in their direction.

"Woah!" Matt cried. "We're friendly."

"How do I know that?" the man hollered. He had thick glasses and a scar on his right cheek. "Seems there aren't many friendly faces around here no more."

"Well, you're looking at some right here," Matt replied, holding his hands out. "Look, I'm not armed."

"He is," the man said, pointing at Tucker.

"Yeah, you're right," Matt agreed. "Kid, why don't you go ahead and put your gun on the ground?"

The teenager eyed the man with suspicion, before reluctantly stooping down and placing his rifle in the dirt.

"There, see? Friendly."

The man turned to his convoy and shrugged. "What do you think?"

"They seem earnest enough," a broad woman with a tangle of gray hair and large eyes replied. "Maybe they know something about what's going on."

Matt approached them. "All we know is, whatever it is, it took down our plane and it seems to have cut off all power and telecommunications in the process."

"We can't contact our kids," an elderly woman cried from the back. "We don't even know if they're okay."

The man in front stuck out his hand. "Name's Patrick," he said.

"I'm Matt, and these people here are all survivors in one way or another."

"I know him," the woman said. "Seen him around town."

"Yeah," Matt replied. "We met Tucker and his dad, Hank, in the mountains. He's gone to look for his wife, Rosie. Seems like she went out and never came home."

"I know her," another woman said. "Rosie Kehrig. Knew her father too, although she was a Bloom then. We were in the same class together."

"Have you seen her since the day before yesterday?" Tucker asked. "I'm real worried about her. My dad, too."

The woman shook her head. "Heck, son. Since everything went to hell, we've just been trying to get by."

Tucker's expression sagged as he turned away. Matt knew the kid was hurting. They all were. Nothing felt real any more, nothing felt sane.

"Where you heading?" Matt asked, watching as a few of the kids started to get restless.

"Anywhere but back there."

"I don't get it. Power's only been down for two days."

"Right," Patrick replied. "But the town already had its troubles. Gangs, drug addicts, and such. It took half a day for those thugs to realize the police were preoccupied, and then the looting started. This here's my family. My wife, my sister and her husband, my cousin Edgar and his brood. We got a place up in the hills, so we're heading there until the worst of it passes."

Matt shook his head, shocked that insanity had bred so quickly. It was as if the whole world had always been on a knife edge, mere seconds from disaster. Perhaps he should have seen it sooner, when he came back from overseas, watching as people blindly led their lives, oblivious to all the evil, deceit, greed, and lust for wealth in the world. The problem with bad guys, they were opportunists, waiting for the market to shift, for the demand to change. Without any authority policing the rules, and without power, light, or any means of transport, the greedy preyed on the weak, picking the carrion as it lay bleeding on the side of the road.

"Well, good luck to you, friend," Matt said. "I hope everything works out for you. For our part, we're gonna forge onward and see if we can find Tucker's mom."

"Best of luck to you, all of you. But don't hang around too long. There's a hell of a storm brewing down there. I wouldn't want to be caught out in the open when the lightning strikes."

"Thanks for the advice," Matt said, watching as the group made their way along the road. "And safe travels."

The town of Emporium was built by settlers in the late 18th century, over a century after William Penn, a renowned Quaker, settled in the area and created what eventually became known as the state of Pennsylvania.

Emporium grew up around the coal mining industry when coal was a booming commodity. The largest mine in the area, Rosetta Pit, sat around 20 miles to the north, and most of the workers lived in Bedford and other larger towns.

However, a local businessman, a banker named Laurence Empor, decided that a settlement up in the mountains, where the air was clean and the land was covered in rich woodland and rolling fields, would make for a nicer, more humble location than the much larger settlements. Consequently, he created the town of Emporium, selling real estate at a fraction of the cost.

His experiment worked to a point, but with the journey to the mine quite hazardous— particularly during the winter months when the roads were covered in snow and thick ice—the residents began to depart in numbers, leaving many of the homes uninhabited.

Empor was subsequently stricken terminally ill with cholera, and with his passing, the land was sold off to Arthur Hodlsworth, a land developer who decided the soil was much better suited for farming. He signed a decree to raze the settlement to the ground. However, Empor's relatives had other ideas, wanting to retain the town of Emporium as their father had pictured it, with its colonial church, picture-perfect town square, and ornate fountain. They fought Holdsworth in court, claiming he had never paid the fee they had agreed when they had decided to sell in full, a court case that lasted until Holdsworth himself passed.

With the development in limbo, even more of the residents left, turning Emporium into a ghost town. The buildings stood empty for years thereafter, dark and lifeless, windows peering silently at streets that once bustled with townsfolk. The civil war raged elsewhere in the state, but Emporium lay untouched, the dust of its past blowing along the sidewalks, coating every surface in a layer of grime.

After the war ended, and with the Industrial Revolution now in full swing, many people began to see the benefit of migrating to the countryside. It was an entrepreneur, Samuel Beckwith, who bought up all the vacant lots and marketed them in the city. Before long, the little town of Emporium had over two thousand residents, and was considered the state's best kept secret, a finely-polished jewel in the Pennsylvanian hills.

Then, the economy crashed and poverty struck, and before long, what had once been an affluent neighborhood, suddenly became a home to drunks, drug addicts, and misfits. Trouble was always just beneath the surface, with secret handshakes on street corners, and intoxicated bodies piled high under sleeping bags and cardboard boxes in store fronts. Maybe in another town, the catastrophic events of that October morning would have had a lesser effect, particularly early on; but, in Emporium, it was the spark that lit the fuse. Sooner or later, something was going to explode.

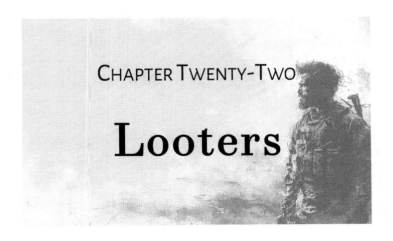

CHAPTER TWENTY-TWO

Looters

They passed a fistfight in the street as a group of kids fought over a box of beer. Further along, they watched as residents nailed timber across the windows of their homes, apparently trying to stave off invaders. Downtown, many of the shop windows had been smashed, and at least three of them had been completely burnt down.

Matt listened as the others gasped, not knowing what to make of such wanton carnage. Gunn's face, in particular, was a picture. The guy looked like he'd stepped onto a movie set and didn't know which way to look.

In the residential neighborhood, things were a little quieter, but even then, the residents watched them eagerly as they passed them by, seemingly relieved that these new visitors weren't trying to kick in their front door. Matt guessed it was like walking along a prison corridor, the inmates glaring out at you, wondering what new hell you were bringing to their pitiful existence.

They arrived at Hank's place a little before noon, and to Tucker's dismay, they found the place deserted. Matt tried the power, but still there was nothing. Geneva tried the phone, but as she raised it to her ear, she shook her head.

"Where are they?" Tucker cried.

"Doesn't mean anything," Matt said. "Could be that your dad's still out there looking for your mom."

It didn't explain Codey's absence, however. Nor did it explain the fact that the door frame still lay in pieces, a victim of his shoulder assault the day prior.

He pointed to Sidney and Otto. "Hey guys," he said. "Get to work on the front door, won't you? I'm going to check in on Roberto and see if he knows anything."

As they rummaged in the downstairs closet for a hammer and nails, Matt crossed the street. The day was overcast, but the rain was holding out, for now at least. There was a chill in the air that had seeped its way through Matt's jacket, into his flesh, and was now coating his bones. He didn't think it was just the weather making him feel that way. Everything was just wrong.

Power cuts didn't last three days in the 21st century, residents didn't feel the need to board up their windows, shopkeepers weren't executed in the street, and planes didn't fall out of the sky. He needed an explanation for what was going on, but he didn't think he was going to find one. They were alone out there, floundering like freshly caught fish, gasping for oxygen.

Roberto came out to greet him as he stepped onto his path. "You made it back," he said. "The others, too."

"Yeah, we decided that Emporium was just one heck of a place to visit." Roberto forced a laugh, but Matt could see the strain etched into his eyes. He looked exhausted, drained. "You okay?" Matt asked. "Something happen?"

"We had some trouble last night," he said. "A few guys, a couple of women. They wanted some of what we had, but I told them I had to feed my children and look after my own. One of the guys took a swing at me, but he'd been drinking, so I managed to land one of my own before they ran off. One of the guys from our neighborhood, Grant Coleman, took one hell of a beating though. They emptied his refrigerator and took all of his canned foods. The residents got together this morning to take some supplies to him and his family. He looked a real mess. I think they broke his nose and cracked a couple of ribs."

Matt groaned. It seemed like the whole town was being overrun by crazies.

"Have you seen Hank?" he asked. "Or Codey?"

Roberto shook his head. "Haven't seen Hank since you left yesterday. Could be he's still out looking for Rosie. Heck, I hope she's okay."

"Yeah," Matt replied, knowing that with every passing hour, the likelihood of a missing person arriving home safely diminished significantly. "And what about Codey? The big fella with the gun."

"Yeah, about him," Roberto said, glancing back toward the house and lowering his voice. "You vouch for him, right?"

Matt didn't like the way Roberto was posing the question. "No, not really. We have a bit of a history." It wasn't entirely the truth, but Matt didn't have the energy to describe to the guy how his girlfriend and her daughter had died in the plane crash that had also almost taken his life, and that Codey was the gangster brother of Lyndsey's recently-deceased husband.

"Right, that makes sense. It's just that—" Robert paused and checked his rear view once more. "He was asking all sorts of crazy stuff."

"Such as?"

"How much ammunition I had, whether I knew who the local gang leaders were, and he asked me which streets in town were the most affluent."

Matt didn't like the sound of that at all. He imagined Codey running the numbers through his own mind, figuring out how quickly he could seize control of a neighborhood and leverage it to his own advantage.

"I can see why you're concerned," he said. "Did you let him inside your house?"

"Yes," Roberto answered, seemingly flustered. "I introduced him to my wife and daughters, and showed him where we stored everything. I thought he was a friend of Hank's."

Matt exhaled slowly. The guy had inadvertently given Codey a guided tour of everything he owned, and what's more, he'd shown him how to get in and out of his property without getting spotted.

"I'd make sure the doors are locked if I were you," Matt said. "And maybe board up your windows, for the time being at least. Maybe this thing will blow over in a day or two, but don't count on it. I've never seen anything like this before, and believe me, I've been involved in some shitshows before. This isn't like anything I've ever experienced. You got water?" Matt asked.

Roberto nodded. "Yeah. Bottled. Enough for a few days."

"I suggest you guard that with your life."

Roberto's expression shifted and his body sagged. "You think this is more than just a power cut, don't you?"

"Oh, this is much more than just a power cut," Matt said, turning and heading back toward the house. "This is something else entirely."

He entered Hank's hallway and surveyed his surroundings. The property was medium in size: three bedrooms, two bathrooms, a large living room, and a kitchen-diner out back. There was a large bay window that faced the street, and two big windows that faced the rear of the property, including two entry points. The garden wasn't fenced off, so it allowed easy access, and the garage was attached to the house via a door that led to the rear of the kitchen. There was a basement beneath their feet, which also had two ground-level windows that opened toward the front of the house. If they were attacked, the building was completely exposed.

He whispered in Otto's ear. "I suggest we make this place safe," he said. "Maybe nobody comes, but maybe somebody does. Roberto tells me Codey's been giving him some strange signals, and my money's on him hooking up with some less than respectable locals. The first place they'll come is a place that he knows."

"The bastard," Otto said. "I never liked that guy."

"Me neither. Are you okay to supervise things here while I head out to see if I can find Hank?"

"Sure thing. You taking the kid?"

"Tucker? Yeah, I think so. He's itching to find his parents, and who can blame him. I'll take Sidney too, and Geneva. That leaves you with Jennifer, Gunn, and Timothy. Will that be okay?"

"Sure. Leave me with the walking wounded, and a guy who looks like he ate through half of Walmart's cold cuts section."

Matt smiled, realizing he'd hardly dealt Otto a fair hand. "We can swap if you like."

Otto shook his head. "It's fine. Go on. I'll make sure we get the job done. Just make sure you bring them back."

Matt withdrew a long blade from a kitchen cabinet and nodded. "Don't worry. I plan to."

They walked into town, passing a dozen or so properties and following a winding path that snaked between a warehouse and a rundown bar. A cop car was parked in the lot, its windows smashed. Inside the building, three men stood motionless, watching them as they passed. One of them was carrying, but the other two looked like they needed a good meal.

"A happy looking bunch," Sidney said. "Do you think they'll come after us?"

Matt tapped the Smith and Wesson .40 handgun that he'd retrieved from Hank's gun closet. "Let's hope not. I wasn't planning on using this thing unless I really have to."

Tucker pulled the strap of his rifle across his shoulder. "If they try anything, I'll take them out with this?"

"You ever shot a person before?" Matt asked, glaring at the boy.

Tucker's cheeks turned crimson. "No, not exactly."

"Not exactly or no? They're not the same thing."

"Then...no."

Matt turned to face him. "Look, kid. I've shot a lot of people, and believe me, I remember every single one. It's not something you take lightly."

"But, what if someone comes at us?"

"Then you make a snap decision, but you make sure it's the right one. If you kill someone, and you find out later that all they wanted was to come and say hi, then you'll never forgive yourself. You get me?"

Tucker glared at him, his gaze steadfast, the corners of his mouth twitching. "I'm not an idiot."

"No," Matt said, recalling Kenzo lying in the dirt, bleeding out while chaos unfolded all around them. "Nobody ever thinks they are."

They rounded a corner and walked out onto a vacant street where a number of abandoned cars littered the road. The main town square was up ahead, and to their right lay the local police station. It was a tiny brick-built building with a tin roof, and the parking lot only had space for one car.

Matt approached the doorway and peered inside. The place looked deserted, as if whoever had manned the desk had decided enough was enough, and upped and left. The door window was cracked, and somebody had obviously gotten inside from the rear, because paperwork was strewn all over the floor, and the filing cabinets had been toppled.

"Where's the law when you need them?" Geneva asked.

"Well, these people have families, too," Matt said. "I'm guessing they wanted to get home and make sure they were safe?"

"And what about the rest of us?" she countered. "Who's looking out for us?"

Matt adjusted his Stetson. "Well, I guess right now, we're looking out for ourselves."

They walked a little further up the street, looking in every store window, checking for signs of life. Nothing stirred. Nobody moved.

"We need supplies," Matt said, turning to Tucker, tossing him a bag. "Grab some bottled water from the store, maybe some beef jerky or food that will keep us for a little while."

He walked toward the center of the square, where the remains of what would have once been an ornate fountain sat, the water no longer running and the pipes rusted and worn.

"Don't think this thing's run for a while." Sidney said. "The whole town looks like it was in need of repair since way before this whole thing went down."

"You got that right," Matt replied, watching as a group crossed the street up ahead. There were four of them, dark shadows with the sun at their back, and they looked like they were heading their way. "Heads up," Matt whispered. "We got company."

Tucker came running out from inside the store. "They don't got much," he said. "And what they got's turning bad, what with the refrigerators being out of action and all. I grabbed some chips, a few cans of beef. There's no water, though. It's all gone."

Matt let out a long breath. He'd suspected as much. With so much uncertainty, he knew people would go for the essentials first—the most essential, of course, being water. Luckily, he'd been taught how to purify rainwater using charcoal as a filtration system, but he knew he'd have to gather the necessary provisions. That was if this whole thing went on much longer, which he suspected it just might.

He'd wanted to get out of the military, to go back to a normal way of life, whatever that was. However, what he was facing right now was so far from normal, it was crazy. Despite his 12-step AA program and the oath he had taken, if he'd been handed a bottle of Jack right there and then, he would have drunk the whole thing without hesitation.

"Wait, I know that guy," Geneva said, watching as the group of three men and one woman approached. "Isn't that—"

"Yep," Matt said, hardly surprised. He'd anticipated this exact moment some time ago. "Hi, Codey," he said. "I see you've made some friends."

"Howdy, cowboy," Codey replied, smiling. "Good to see you all made it back safely. While you were out there on your little hike through the mountains, I thought I'd widen our network a little bit. You know, safety in numbers?"

Matt eyed the others in turn. The two guys looked similar, as if they were brothers. They had shifty eyes and wiry frames. The taller one had long hair, cut into a mullet, and the shorter one had a long beard and shaved head. The woman had blond pigtails but a yellow, heavily lined face, as if she'd smoked too much reefer.

"Did you find Hank?" Matt asked.

"Who? Oh, you mean the old guy?" Codey replied, half smirking. "Nah. I'm betting he's taken off."

"What?!" Tucker cried. "He wouldn't do that."

"Well, look around you, kid," Codey said. "You see him?"

Matt watched Tucker's expression shift as he thought about fighting his corner, but then pulled back, shrinking as if the weight of everything was just about crushing his thin frame.

"The kid's right," Matt said. "Hank wouldn't have done that."

"If you say so," Codey sniped. "Anyway, me and my new friends here, we got a business proposition for you."

"I don't deal with people I don't know," Matt replied. "So, perhaps, you should introduce me."

Codey slapped his forehead. "Yeah, right. Well, this here is the lovely Jemima."

"Gemma!" the woman hissed. "How many times I gotta tell you? It's Gemma."

"That's right, sorry. This is Gemma. And these two guys are the Cox brothers. Tall one's Levi, short one's Lonnie."

The two guys nodded but didn't speak.

"Where did you find them?" Matt asked.

"No matter," Codey replied. "All you gotta know is these guys have connections with the right people. The sort of people who can get you what you need to stay alive."

Matt let out a long breath. "So, basically you've hooked up with some lowlife looters."

"Who you calling *looters*?" Levi yelled, missing the real insult. "We don't take nothing that's not freely available."

"You mean available at the end of a rifle," Geneva said, "or with its rightful owner bruised and battered into submission?"

"Who's the old bitch?" Lonnie hissed. "You wanna go back to your whorehouse, bitch?"

"Give me that!" Geneva yelled, reaching for Tucker's gun. "I'm gonna blow this dipshit's head off!"

Matt reached out a hand and pulled the gun away, leaving Geneva red-faced and blowing heavily.

"I gotta say," he said. "I don't much like your new friends' people skills."

"I didn't recruit them for their people skills," Codey replied, no longer smiling. "I recruited them because they can get me what I need."

Matt glanced at Sidney, whose finger was hovering mere inches above his own weapon—a Colt that he had located beneath some junk in Hank's garage—and at Tucker, who was itching for a fight. Not to mention Geneva, who looked like she was just about ready to blow a gasket.

"We're gonna go," Matt said. "Continue our search. I recommend you don't come back to the house Codey, or your pals. Seems to me you've chosen a different path."

Codey's face remained impassive. "Don't mean the roads we're on won't come together eventually," he said. "You and me have some history that needs settling."

"I look forward to that," Matt said, his tone calm but menacing. "Whenever you're ready, I'll be waiting."

As they walked away, leaving Codey and his new pals standing in the dust, Matt knew he had a new problem he was going to have to deal with—a problem that needed resolving once and for all.

CHAPTER TWENTY-THREE

Phoenix

That afternoon, after they'd abandoned the search for the day, Matt called a meeting with the residents of Hank's street—Mayflower Avenue. Around 50 people attended in all, including Roberto, his wife and kids, the survivors from the downed 737, and seven other households. They assembled on Hank's front lawn, their faces anxiously anticipating what this guy wearing the cowboy hat and leather boots was going to say. Somehow he'd taken on the role of leader of the neighborhood, which seemed ludicrous to him. However, the people needed someone to do something, because doing something meant that, just maybe, it wasn't the end of the world.

"If y'all are hanging out for the authorities to arrive, I suggest you think again," Matt began. "We've seen the police station here in town, and it's been abandoned."

"Sheriff Hanson wouldn't leave us like that," one of the mothers said. "She grew up in this community."

"Well, I don't know what to tell y'all," Matt replied. "She's not there."

"He's right," Tucker added. "Car's been pretty smashed up too, like someone took an iron bar to it or something."

There was a groan from the gathering, and one of the women burst into tears.

"I guess, what I'm saying," Matt continued, "is if we're going to get through this, hold out until the military takes charge of the situation, then we're going to have to coordinate our efforts and look out for each other. Sitting in our own houses, protecting what's our own without consideration for your neighbor, that's just not gonna cut it."

"So, what do we do?" one of the men asked. He was a tall, middle-aged man with a tangled mop of hair. He didn't like the kind of guy who could even begin to put up a fight.

"We fortify our homes," Matt said. "We pool our provisions. If somebody we don't know walks along the road, we signal each other. We figure out a way of purifying the water, and we share what we have."

"I got four kids!" a woman yelled. "I can't afford to give away any food."

"I'm not asking you to give it away," Matt replied. "I'm suggesting we pool and ration it. That way, it'll last longer and it will buy us some time."

He thought he sounded like a school principal, firing off instructions as if he had any right to boss these people around, but the simple fact was, he knew what he was talking about. He had the training. From the look of the people standing waiting on his every word, he was the only that had the skills required to drag them, kicking and screaming, through this hell.

"What about guns? Ammunition?" an older guy shouted. "I've only got a pea-shooter compared to some of the weapons I know you all have."

"In the word of truth, in the power of God; by the weapons of righteousness for the right hand and the left," Matt said, caressing the handle of his Smith and Wesson.

"What?" the man replied. "You a God fearing man, son?"

"More than that," Matt replied. "I put my faith in him, and I think he puts his faith in me, too, even though I've strayed from the flock more times than I care to mention."

"God's not going to save us," a woman hollered. "If he was, why'd he let this happen in the first place?"

Matt took a moment to consider his response. He'd had the same thoughts, particularly when he'd lost people, good people, but he also knew that becoming cynical, just because your life hadn't been a pathway paved with gold, was a surefire route straight to hell.

"Well, we'll only find the answer to that question when we stand before our Lord Almighty, and when we do, he will bless us with his sacred hand, and then we will know. We will know everything."

The crowd fell silent. The only sound was the whistling of the wind through the leaves of the tall trees, and the sound of the children growing impatient.

"Look," Matt said. "Put your faith in me, and in my friends here, and we'll do what we can to make sure Emporium withstands the storm. But you need to spread the word to people you know in town. We're going to need everybody onside if we're going to get through what's coming, because there's the devil at the gate, and believe me, he won't back down without a fight."

Matt sat at the dining room table, loading and reloading his gun. He hadn't slept all night, couldn't sleep. He kept seeing Codey's face in his dreams, but it wasn't Codey at all. It was someone who looked just like him. It was only when this new version of Codey turned around, and he saw he had his arm around Lyndsey, that he realized it was Codey's brother, Mason. He had a look on his face that spelled trouble, as if he was itching for a fight. Lyndsey shrunk beside him, her shoulders hunched, her expression one of reluctant acceptance.

"Get your hands away from her," dream-Matt yelled. "In the name of his Lord Almighty, I will kill you if you touch her, you sonofabitch."

Mason turned to Lyndsey, as if she had said something he didn't like, and shoved her to the ground, looming over her like a silverback, his fists clenched. Matt reached for the gun in his belt, but it wasn't there, so he picked up a rock.

"Get away from her!"

When he looked down at Lyndsey, he realized it wasn't Lyndsey at all. It was Tiffany, and she was holding her stomach where the bulge of an as yet unborn son was visible. She was dressed in a figure hugging skirt and high heels, and her makeup was expertly applied. She turned toward Matt and grinned, blood running from her sharpened teeth.

"No!" he cried, "leave my boy alone."

And that was when he sat up, sweat pouring from his face and beard, his body drenched.

Sitting there at the table, focusing on what he could control, he thought of the townsfolk, of the respect they had shown for him. Sure, they were uncertain, afraid, and perhaps mistrustful of the newcomers who had shown up at their door, claiming they could protect them, but Matt had a calling. For the first time since he'd arrived back from Iraq, he felt useful. He liked Emporium, especially the lay of the land, the smallness of it, and the comforts. Sure, it was in the grip of tyranny, violence, and selfish greed, but he had never backed down from a fight, and he wasn't about to start now.

Otto and the others had done a good job of repairing the place, as well as fortifying the windows and entrance points. Matt thought it would take one hell of an attack for the house to be breached without them knowing it. They had a few weapons, which would stave off a small force, but if a larger group came at them, he knew they would be in trouble. He thought his call to the community to pool their weapons would help resolve that issue, but only if everybody complied.

He thought of the oath he made to himself in the mountains, sitting by the covered bodies of Lyndsey and A.J. He'd had enough of putting the whole world before himself. He was going to look out for number one. But, what if looking out for number one could be combined with protecting the townsfolk and, at the same time, gaining a position of authority in the community where he could put his skills as a soldier and preacher to good use?

As he mulled everything over, he took a metal scribe he'd located in the workshop and began to write a verse from scripture on the handle of his weapon. It was one he had used on countless occasions to signify strength and fortitude.

Matthew 10:34, "Do not think that I came to bring peace on earth; I did not come to bring peace, but a sword."

These people needed a sword, but more than that, they needed somebody who was prepared to wield it. He was not afraid to be that person, and if Codey and his cronies came knocking, he would bring the blade down with everything he had.

As the sun began to rise over the horizon, there was a pounding on the front door. Matt leapt up from the table, his gun in his hands. He stood in the hallway and listened keenly for any further sounds. Jennifer descended the stairs, holding the handrail with her good hand, and glared at him.

"Who is it?" she whispered.

He shrugged, just as the pounding recommenced. Jennifer let out a tiny shriek before backing away.

"Wait here," he said, before heading to the door. He peeked through the side window, pulling the blinds aside, before letting out, "What the heck?"

He opened the door wide, letting the meager sunlight in, and looked up at the giant beast that stood before him. It had a chestnut coat, a nose like velvet, and dark eyes that seemed to peer into his very soul.

"Well, hello there, fella," he said, as the horse whinnied. Behind it, a woman stood. She was the stout lady from the group the night before. She was grinning, and standing with another horse by her side, this one dark gray in color.

"We spoke last night," Matt said. "You were commenting about food for your kids."

"I was," the woman said. "Name's Savannah. I run the stables around here, and you looked like a guy who could use some transport. That is, if you plan on sticking around."

"I do," Matt said, unable to take his eyes off the horse's glimmering coat.

"His name is Phoenix," Savannah said. "And he's been bugging me to find him an owner who could use him just as much as he wants to be used." Savannah had already taken the opportunity to saddle the horse, and she gestured for Matt to hitch himself up. "Have you ever ridden a horse before, Matt?" she asked.

"Ma'am," Matt replied. "I'm from Tennessee. Horses are a way of life."

"Then, you and Phoenix here will be fast friends," she replied. "Now, I have someone I'd like you to meet. You want to take a ride on Phoenix with me and my horse, Blackhawk, here?"

Matt eyed Jennifer, who was now standing beside him. "Get the others to work on that water filtration system we spoke about," he said to the younger woman. "I'll be back before you know it."

Riding Phoenix felt like getting back on a motorcycle after years of inactivity—it was as instinctive as breathing or sitting behind the wheel of a favorite car. His muscles were taut beneath his thighs, and while the horse fought him at first, he soon complied with Matt's every wish, moving the way he wanted and almost becoming at one with him. They sped through the streets, passing burned out vehicles, broken front doors, and dumpsters on their side, spewing trash onto the road. It was as though lawlessness was now the only way of life in Emporium, as if everything people had learned at school about what was right and wrong had been discarded and meant nothing all along.

At the base of a hill stood a large, Victorian house with black windows and sweeping verandas. It looked like it had seen better days, as if its inhabitants had aged with it and failed to keep up with the maintenance, but it still remained an impressive property.

Savannah dismounted Blackhawk and knocked on the door. Matt also dismounted his own horse and stood beside her.

"Who lives here?" he asked, but before he could answer, an elderly woman opened the door and peered up at him.

"Who's this?" she asked Savannah, with a voice that sounded like broken glass.

"Somebody who thinks he can help us," she said. "He's from the southern states."

"Tennessee," Matt added. "The name's Matthew Groover, but you can call me Matt." He held out a hand and the old lady took it. Her bones felt tiny and hollow like a bird's.

"This, here, is the town elder," Savannah said. "She's lived here longer than anybody else, isn't that right?"

The old woman smiled. Her eyes were like tiny pin pricks, her mouth small and surrounded by deep crevices. "The name's Isla," she said, "but, for years, people just call me "the elder," as if I'm so old, they can't even remember my name."

"It's good to meet you," Matt said. "And I'll call you whatever you want me to, ma'am. I got no ax to grind either way."

"Well, then," she said. "You might as well go along with all the others. Don't make no difference to me."

Matt turned his attention to Savannah. "Is there something you wanted me to discuss with the elder?"

"Nope," Savannah replied. "Just get her approval. If you're gonna be heading up whatever it is you want us to do to keep ourselves safe, I wanted the elder to know, that's all."

"And what is it you plan to do?" the elder asked, watching as Matt adjusted his hat. "This ain't no cow-rustling town, and it ain't the Wild West either. You can't go shooting people just because they don't fit in."

"No," Matt replied, placing his hand on his weapon. "But we can defend ourselves. With force, if necessary."

"You a military boy, Matt?" the elder asked.

"Why do you ask that?"

"Because you look like you know how to fight."

Matt allowed a smile to creep across his face. "Well, I guess I do, ma'am."

She went to him then, placing her hand on his forearm and peering into his eyes. "Then, you fight for Emporium and you fight for these people. They're good, for the most part, but they need protecting. They ain't never known a situation like this—hell, I don't think anybody has—but these folks more than most. They need leading, Matt, and I don't have the energy left in my old body to take on that responsibility. If you've got what it takes, then I say, do whatever you need to."

"I'll do what I can."

The elder looked at him, her eyes steely and fierce, and then turned to Savannah.

Her chin jutted forward as she raised her head, her white hair framing her thin face. "He has my approval."

CHAPTER TWENTY-FOUR

Chase the Wolves

On the ride back, they passed Codey, the Cox brothers, and a few of the others. They were hauling liquor from a warehouse and loading a wagon that was hitched to two skinny looking donkeys. Codey looked up at him as they rode past and cocked his finger, as if firing an imaginary bullet in his direction.

When they arrived back at the house, Otto was directing the others, using instructions Matt had provided him the day prior. The town of Emporium sat beside the river Sable which wound its way down through the mountains, and via a means of purifying through charcoal—a stock of which one of the other residents directed them to—Matt wagered that they would be able to clean enough river and rainwater to sustain the town for the foreseeable future.

The apparatus was some way off completion, but it was good to see the residents together, doing something for the common good. It was as though this simple act gave the locals something to focus on to ease their spirits. Matt had seen the same in the military. The men would always joke and laugh when they had a task to complete, but when there was nothing to do, the mood darkened and black thoughts crept in.

With the horses hitched to a nearby tree, Matt turned his attention to Tucker, who was sitting with his head between his knees by the side of the house.

"You okay, kid?"

Tucker shook his head, and when he peered up at him through red-rimmed eyes, Matt knew he had been crying.

"Where are they?" he asked. "They've been gone for days."

Matt shook his head. He wished he had the answers. "I don't know, Tuck. But you have to keep hoping. You have to have faith."

"And look where that's got me," he said. "Before this happened, I had a mom and dad. I had a good life, good prospects. I was doing pretty good in school. All that's gone now. All that's—"

The kid broke down again, and Matt gestured for Gunn to come over. "Can you sit with him?" he asked, knowing that Gunn had more things in common with the youngster than he ever could. "Talk to him?"

Gunn nodded. "Sure thing."

Matt went to Otto who was barking orders at two of the younger men. Matt wondered if the old guy had been a factory supervisor before things had turned sour, as he seemed to like being in charge.

"I've been thinking about our predicament," Matt said. "If this is going to go the way I think it is, we could be up here in the mountains for a long time with no help on the horizon."

Otto wiped sweat from his brow as his eyes narrowed. "How so?"

"If they were coming, they would be here already or we would have heard something."

Otto nodded. "Yeah, I guess you're right. So, what are you thinking?"

Matt gestured toward the one road in and out that dissected the town in two. "I think we have to defend our location in some way."

"You mean fence ourselves in?" Matt nodded his head, drawing in the dirt with a stick. He sketched the church, the square in the middle of town with the rusted up fountain, the shopping district, and the four main blocks that made up the residential area. At the upper most corner, he drew the Victorian mansion where the elder lived. "That's a pretty good likeness," Otto said. "You ever work as an architect?"

"I'm a soldier, Otto," Matt replied, grinning. "Not an artist." He sketched in the mountains that surrounded them, the valley that lay beneath them, the river that ran along the eastern edge of the land, and the woodland that lay to the south. "We're exposed," he said. "On all sides. Our only strength is that we're on—"

"Higher ground," Otto replied. "If gangs made their way here from the other towns, they'd have to come at us from the valley."

"Right," Matt interjected. "So, if we put sentry points here, here, here, and here," he drew watchtowers at the four corners of the settlement, "we should see them coming from two, maybe three, miles away."

Otto grinned, peering down at the rough sketch in the dirt. "You think we should connect the towers with some sort of fence?"

Matt thought about that for a moment. "I think that would be a good idea."

"It's going to take a lot of timber and a lot of effort."

Matt gestured toward the forest, and then at the residents who were helping construct the filtration system. "These people are keen, and we have the resources."

There was a sound like a gun being discharged from some way off in the distance, and the residents stopped what they were doing, waiting for something to go down. There was the sound of another shot, followed by a man yelling.

"The only problem we have," Matt said, "is we don't want to cage ourselves in with the wolves."

"Meaning what exactly?" Otto replied.

Matt adjusted his stetson and eyed his pistol. "Meaning we gotta chase the wolves from our door, and make damn sure they never come back."

Matt and Otto rode Phoenix and Blackhawk respectively toward the town square, Matt carrying his Smith and Wesson and Otto carrying the Colt that Sidney had located. As they approached, there was the sound of further gunfire, and a noise like a woman screaming. There was smoke billowing from one of the houses, followed by the sound of a roof caving in. As they neared, laughter filled the air. It was cruel and malicious, as if a group of hyenas were circling a stricken herd.

"This don't sound good," Otto said.

Matt nodded. It reminded him of Iraq, when the AQI would round up American sympathizers and taunt them in the streets, prodding, probing, and assaulting them before stripping them naked and executing them. It was inhumane and barbaric, but it happened on a regular basis. This sounded just like that, sending his brain back to that hellhole of a sandbox, but he shook it away, trying to remain in the present.

They cantered down the street, passing the church that had been vandalized almost beyond repair, past the shops that had been looted and damaged, their windows shattered and doors kicked in, and beyond the police station that lay deserted and silent.

In the middle of the square, by the derelict fountain, sat a man, bloodied and battered, his face a mask of cuts and swellings. Beside him lay the body of another woman with hazel curls and a button nose. There was a hole between her eyes where a bullet had penetrated. Around them stood the Cox brothers, Gemma with the yellow face and vacant stare, and two other men.

"Wait," Otto said. "Isn't that man..?"

Matt nodded, feeling his stomach burn with hatred. "Yeah. That's Hank alright."

"Shit," Otto hissed. "Do you think that's his wife lying dead on the ground?"

Matt blew through his teeth. *Yeah, that was exactly what he thought.* He recalled Tucker sitting with his head between his knees and knew he couldn't let him lose two parents in one day.

"You take the window up there," Matt said, pointing toward the butcher shop. "You cover me if things go south."

Otto didn't need a second invitation, and he dismounted his horse and moved as fast as his aging frame would allow him. Matt watched him disappear into the store. If he was going to be in charge of the place, he was going to need a strong second, and despite his senior years, Otto was both dependable and hardworking. He fit the bill entirely. They'd been thrown together by tragic circumstances, but they'd forged a friendship and an understanding that Matt valued. He was going to need someone to watch his back.

He rode toward the group, watching as the taller of the brothers, Levi, nudged his shorter brother, Lonnie, and gestured toward Matt.

"Well, lookee here," Lonnie said, "If it ain't that cowboy that Codey introduced us to a while back. Howdy doody, cowboy. You wanna come join in the fun?"

Matt glanced at the woman on the floor, blood seeping from the hole in her head and the exploded skull at the back, her brain splattered on the concrete. Hank looked up at him through swollen eyes, his nose fractured and cheek bruised. He looked like he'd taken one hell of a beating, but worse than that, it looked like his soul had been drained from his body.

"What's going on here?" he asked.

"These two went where they didn't belong," Gemma said, her voice hissing and spiteful like a spitting snake.

"And where exactly is that?"

"They were taking our supplies," Lonnie said. "Stealing from us."

"My wife was hurt," Hank said through swollen lips. "She'd been attacked. She needed bandages, antiseptic."

Matt stared at the woman's body and the laceration across her abdomen. He put the pieces together.

Somebody had assaulted her in the hours after the event and Hank had found her, bloodied and possibly unconscious. He'd gone to find supplies, but had inadvertently stepped into a whole load of trouble—trouble that was now fronted by none other than Lyndsey's violent brother-in-law.

"You was stealing!" Gemma yelled. "Like a dirty thief."

"Well, hang on there," Matt said. "Didn't ya'll steal those things in the first place?"

"He's trying to be a wise ass," Levi said, moving his hand to his weapon. "You don't wanna be doing that, fella."

"Watch where you're placing that hand," Matt said, shooting a glance toward the darkened window above the butcher's shop and spying Otto up there, his gun aimed at the taller of the two brothers.

"Or what?" he said. "There's five of us and just one of you, not counting him." He pointed to Hank, laughing. "And I'm pretty sure he wet his pants when I shot his wife."

"You bastard," Hank hissed. "You killed my Rosie. You killed the mother of my son."

"*You killed the mother of my son, you killed the mother of my son,*" Gemma said in a sing-song voice, mocking him. "You gonna cry, man?"

"I suggest you leave him be," Matt said. "I think it's best if you be on your way."

Lonnie glared at his brother. "This guy's trying to give us orders?"

"Sounds like it," Levi said. "You ain't the boss around here."

"Maybe not the boss," Matt replied, looking at them each in turn, weighing up how quickly he could draw his weapon and take them down. He knew it wouldn't be anywhere near quick enough, but luckily he had Otto watching his every move. "But I've told the people of this town that we'll make things right around here, and that means this shit has to stop. Right...now."

"Ha," Gemma squealed. "What a joke. How are you gonna do that, cowboy? Ride into town and shoot up all the bad guys."

"If that's what it takes," he said.

The four men turned to face him, their fingers resting on their guns. "Well, if you're gonna do that,"

Lonnie said, "you're gonna have to be pretty fast with the trigger."

"Yes, sir," Matt replied. "Looks that way."

The wind blew down the street, tossing empty cans along the sidewalk, the rattle of tin against stone sounding like gunfire in the distance. Matt watched the men, saw the way they were standing, nervousness in their eyes. They sensed Matt was more than just an ordinary citizen, but they had their orders to kill Hank and his wife to send a message to the other residents that their stock was not to be touched, and they had to follow through with it.

Levi winked at his brother, and the men reached for their guns, but Matt was quick, letting off two shots before dismounting Phoenix, chasing him away before moving behind the fountain. Above them, Otto let off a volley of shots, taking down two of the guys, and hitting the woman high in the thigh.

"Shit!" she yelled. "Somebody shot me."

Levi and Lonnie had scattered, but Matt managed to take aim and put one in Lonnie's back as he made for one of the stores. He went down hard, his face connecting with the sidewalk with a smack. Levi was quicker, however, and he positioned himself behind an abandoned vehicle, letting off half a dozen shots that struck the fountain on either side of Matt.

Hank lay on the ground, trying to protect his wife's body with his own. Matt thought about that, the senselessness of it. Rosie was already dead, her brains blown clean out of her head. Yet, her husband of many years was hellbent on making sure no bullets struck her body, even if it meant getting shot himself.

"For God's sake, Hank, get over here!" Matt yelled. "I'll cover you." Hank didn't move. His back shuddered as he sobbed, grieving for the loss of a woman he deeply loved. "Hank! Come on, man! We'll do the right thing when this is over, but right now, we need to focus on staying alive!"

Hank lay there as bullets whistled by mere inches from his body.

"Tucker needs you!" Matt yelled, which seemed to jar Hank into action. He looked up, kissed his wife's blood soaked hair, and rolled across the ground, coming to rest beside Matt.

"How many?" Hank asked, his voice hoarse.

"Two, I think," Matt said, gesturing up the hill. "The tall guy and the woman, although I think she's been wounded pretty badly."

As if to highlight the point, Gemma rose from behind another vehicle and fired toward the window where Otto was hiding, striking the frame and sending shards of timber flying in all directions. Otto stood and returned fire, hitting the woman in the shoulder, and then, fatally, one in her eyeball. She flopped to the ground, lifeless, a bloody hole where her eye had once been.

"There's one left," Hank said. "And he's the one that shot my Rosie. Let me take him, Matt."

Matt glared at his weapon, and then up at Hank's mess of a face. "I don't think so, Hank."

"Please," he said, his voice steeped in emotion. "I have to avenge her...her death."

Matt could see how distraught Hank was, and he reluctantly handed the gun to him. "You sure you're up to this?"

Hank didn't answer. He merely stood and opened fire, putting four bullets into the ground where Levi was hiding.

"Careful," Matt said. "We're running low on ammo."

Levi peeked out from behind the vehicle and fired at Hank, but his aim was off, missing by a couple of feet.

"You bastard!" Hank roared. "You shot Rosie, you sonofabitch!" He paced toward the vehicle, letting off shot after shot, but Levi was smart and wedged himself behind the fender, ensuring the bullets missed their mark. Hank danced around the front of the car, catching Levi off guard, and he grinned as he took aim. Matt heard the click of the hammer as it slammed against the mechanism repeatedly, and looked up to see Hank's bemused expression. The gun was empty. "Shit."

Levi stood, a broad smile across his lips, and raised his own gun. "If you're gonna come after a wolf, my friend, you better have a better aim."

Just as he was about to pull the trigger, there was a crack from high above him and a bullet whistled past his ear and hit the barrel of the handgun, throwing it into the air. Levi leapt, shaking his hand as if he had been shot, and peered up at Otto, who held a smoking

Colt in his grip. The old boy smiled at Matt, raising his thumb and winking, but then the shadows behind him began to take a shape and a face emerged; round with a crooked nose, short, dark hair, platinum rings on his fingers, and a sneer that screamed hatred and vengeance.

As the knife slipped across Otto's throat and the blood sprayed from the window, Matt screamed out and dove for Hank, grabbing his shoulders and pulling him away before Levi could collect his gun. He took the Smith and Wesson and slammed home a fresh magazine, letting off a volley of shots and pushing Hank toward Phoenix. As he turned, he watched as Otto toppled from the window, his body smashing onto the ground with a sickening thud.

Codey stood at the opening, casually wiping the fresh blood from his knife and laughing, watching as Matt pulled himself up onto the horse and tugged on the reins.

"Ride, Phoenix!" he yelled, catching a glimpse of Otto's lifeless body and feeling the acidic heat of anger building in his gut. "For God's sake, ride!"

CHAPTER TWENTY-FIVE

The Crescent

Matt dragged Hank back into the house, his face bloodied and tears pouring from his eyes. Tucker came out to meet them and grabbed his father, holding him just about as tight as another human could withstand. Matt watched as Hank initially resisted the embrace, not knowing whether to celebrate his reunion with his only son or grieve the wife he had just lost, but eventually he lifted his arms to hug Tucker and sobbed into his shoulder.

"I'm sorry, son," he said. "I'm so sorry."

Tucker began to cry then, realizing that his mother was never coming home.

"What happened?" he asked through the tears. "Who did it?"

Geneva and the others approached, cautiously at first, but when they saw what was happening, a huddle quickly formed, with the grieving pair at its center. Matt watched in silence, thinking of Otto and how he had inadvertently sent the old man to his death. Codey must have been up there all along, anticipating what was to come. Matt had let his friend walk straight into a trap, one that he would never return from.

"Wait?" Gunn said. "Where's Otto?"

The group turned and looked at Matt, anticipating an answer. After a moment, he shook his head. "There were five of them," he said. "We didn't know that bastard was up there. I sent Otto into the store to provide some cover, but he was waiting."

"Otto's dead?" Jennifer asked, tears welling in her eyes.

Matt nodded. "He died a hero's death. Rescued Hank here from a bullet."

Hank nodded. "They shot Rosie in cold blood," he added. "Didn't show any remorse, any compassion. They're evil. *That man is evil!*"

He and his son looked like their whole world had been taken from them, as if the ground had evaporated at their feet.

"What do we do next?" Geneva asked, her eyes red with tears.

"We get ready," Matt said. "They'll be coming here next."

Roberto helped gather as many residents as possible, and they stood on the lawn, their ammunition and weapons piled in a heap in the center. The elder was there, as was Savannah and her family, the other residents of Mayflower Avenue, as well as a whole bunch of people Matt had yet to be acquainted with. It didn't matter. They had one shot at defending their homes and protecting their families, and they needed every man and woman to do whatever it took to achieve that one singular goal.

"This street will be our defensive base," Matt said, knowing that concentrating their efforts into one small area gave them the best shot of overcoming the approaching army. "Sidney and Timothy will help with any fortifications. We've got enough disused cars, tires, and junk to build ourselves some cover along this road. With the guns that we have, we should be able to arm each post."

"How many of them are there?" the elder asked.

Matt shook his head. He didn't know. He'd only ever seen Codey with a few goons, but that didn't mean he hadn't recruited a whole load of others with similar mindsets who thought the best way to overcome adversity was to take what other people had, by force if necessary.

"How many residents are missing?" he countered, looking at the 80 or so people who had gathered to listen.

One of the men stood up. "Maybe 50 or so," he said. "Possibly more. There's a rumor that a few men from Huntsville heard what was going on here and made their way across."

Matt puffed out his cheeks. He didn't like the sound of that. A well-armed militia of 50 people would be tough to overcome. However, if they'd managed to boost their numbers by allowing in outsiders, then their chances of success were rapidly dwindling.

"Well," he said, attempting to sound confident. "We still outnumber them, and we have home advantage. That outta count for something."

"Depends on how many guns they have," the man replied. "And, from what I've heard, they've got a lot."

There was a murmuring among the crowd as a nervous anxiety pervaded the air.

"We're running low on rations," a woman yelled. "And water, too. How are we supposed to survive?"

The noise was gathering momentum now, as was the unrest. "We have the charcoal purification system," Matt said, trying to appease them. "It will take a few days to get up and running, but once it does, the rainwater and the river water combined will give us enough to make sure everybody has water to drink. And, as for food, I hear that Codey and his men have a warehouse that has enough food to keep us going for a while. Afterward, if the authorities haven't managed to fix this mess, we'll hunt."

"That's assuming we're not all killed first!"

Matt found himself starting to get irritated. He was trying to give these people hope, exhibit the leadership skills he'd learned in the military, trying to find some way to help these folks survive, and yet they were throwing everything he said back at him as if he were the cause of everything that had gone wrong in the preceding few days. He'd lost, too. *He'd lost everything.*

"Maybe we should surrender," a woman suggested. "If the odds are stacked against us, I mean." She held her son close to her. "I'd rather accept defeat and live, than fight and die."

Matt couldn't believe what he was hearing. He saw what those men had done to Rosie, what Codey had done to his friend, Otto.

"Look at this," he said, raising his Smith and Wesson. "Wherefore take unto you the whole armor of God, that you may be able to withstand in the evil day, and having done all, to stand."

"What the hell's that supposed to mean?" one of the younger men yelled.

"That we have faith on our side, the power of our one true savior. I know many of you believe, but for some of you, your belief is waning. I can tell you that through the hardships in my life, He has always been there. Even when my faith lapsed, He never left me. When the outlook was grim and the way ahead was dark, He stood next to me, shoulder to shoulder, arm in arm, showing me the way. Never has my God abandoned me. Never has He left me alone in the wilderness, wondering which way to turn. I may have strayed, I may have walked a path that was not meant to be walked upon, but He didn't judge me. He didn't close his eyes and turn away."

There was hushed silence.

"We will make it through this," Matt said. "We will succeed. I'm not going to lie to you, all of you. It will be tough, we will lose some people, of that I have no doubt. But, if we stand together—if we stay unified and commit to our purpose—we will emerge through that wall of fire righteous and victorious. He will make it so."

As he spoke, Sidney, Timothy, Gunn, Geneva, and Jennifer came to stand beside him, linking arms, forming a long, unified line. Gradually, others joined: a wounded Hank and his son; Rodney and his family;

Savannah, her husband, and children; and even the elder, who had been standing silently as she watched the mood shift among the crowd. Seeing so many people aligning with Matt's words, a few of the others joined too, forming a large crescent that stretched from Hank's house, all the way to the sidewalk, and along the street. Eventually, almost everyone had joined him, with just a few stragglers standing motionless on the lawn, wondering where best to place their chips. A couple wandered off, unable to fully commit to what was to come, but most stayed.

"We fight this fight," Matt said, his voice cracked with emotion. "But we will win. I tell you this as I stand here as your leader, we will be victorious."

CHAPTER TWENTY-SIX

Mortal Danger

The night came and went, and Matt sat on the porch, his guns on the table beside him. Hank had seen that Matt had commandeered his Smith and Wesson, and he gave him another from his collection. It seemed as though the guy really did have an admirable stash of fine weapons.

The moon hung overhead like a milky eye, watching as Mayflower Avenue became a fortress of sorts: the road littered with abandoned cars, stacks of tires, and assorted junk meant to provide cover for their defensive positions. They had no explosives, no ability to create booby traps as such, but Matt had a plan. He only hoped that it would be good enough.

He considered Codey, of how swiftly he had switched allegiances and turned everything to his advantage. If Lyndsey's husband, Mason, had been anything like his brother, then he knew that her life would have been all flavors of hell. Codey had no moral code or ethical boundaries. He knew one thing and one thing only, and that was how to get the most from any given situation regardless of how it affected others. Rosie had been a victim of that, as had Otto, Lyndsey, and her daughter. He would pay for what he had done, Matt would see to it personally.

The air was crisp, and a dampness lurked in the atmosphere, invading Matt's clothes and seeping through to his skin. He didn't feel it, though. He thought of his journey from Iraq to his hometown, from his mother and father to his real parents who he never knew, from the bottom of a whiskey bottle to the door of the church, from Tiffany to Lyndsey, from Tennessee to Emporium. He wasn't going to stumble at the last second and let that fool stop him from taking his position of power.

Sure, he hadn't counted on leading a band of civilians into battle. He hadn't counted on his plane falling out of the sky either, but that didn't make it any less true. He'd stumbled through his existence, wondering what it was that would set him apart from other men, give him a true purpose, and help him focus his talents on something worthwhile—something that he would be remembered for.

Sure, he'd found God again, and he'd initially thought that was his big revelation—his big moment of clarity—but perhaps that was just a catalyst, a footstep in the sand, leading him to this one moment of lasting and eternal epiphany. Maybe the whole world had gone to hell, maybe things would return to normal or maybe they wouldn't; but right now, right at that exact moment and for a duration to be determined, these people needed a leader. If that meant, when all was said and done, he would be the person to guide them through the fiery gates of the world below, then so be it. If the burden was his to bear, then he would carry it on his shoulders like a child from a burning building. His will would not be quashed, his determination would not waiver.

"Anything?" Hank asked, his face still swollen and his right eye almost closed.

Matt shook his head. "Thanks for the extra gun," he said, pointing to his weapons.

"Heck," Hank replied, taking a seat beside him. "The first one looked so good in your hand, I thought you may as well have the pair."

Matt looked across at him. "How you holding up?"

"I've had better days."

"And Tucker?"

"He's asleep. I think not knowing where we were, then seeing me all beaten up, and learning about his mother's—" he paused to collect himself. "You know, I think it's taken the strength out of him."

"We're gonna need him," Matt said. "You think he'll be up to it?"

Hank nodded, gripping his rifle. "If it means avenging the death of his mother, he'll be just fine. He's a good shot, and he has a steady hand."

Matt watched as a few of the others put the finishing touches to a wall of tires at the point where the street curved to the left. "It's gonna be a fight to the death," he said. "It's not gonna be pretty."

Hank's face split into a bloodied grin. "Do I look like someone who cares about whether something's pretty, Matt?"

Matt laughed, pulling his jacket around his chest. "No, I guess not."

When the laughter subsided, Hank leaned forward in his chair. "What happens next?"

"What do you mean?"

"Well, assuming we get through this, what's after that? How long can we hold out before someone else comes knocking? If it really is as bad out there as they say it is, we could be living this hell for months, maybe a year. There's other Codey's out there, others like the Cox brothers, wanting to take what's ours, burn down our homes, and destroy our families. How the hell are we gonna stop the bad guys from winning?"

Matt had thought about that, and he recalled the conversation he'd had with Otto. "We're gonna build ourselves an enclosure," he said after a moment. "Not around the whole town, but around the core of it, big enough to house maybe a hundred, a hundred and fifty people."

"Like a fort?"

"Yeah, kinda like that. We're gonna have to make some decisions about who we can trust, who can stay, and who has to go. We'll have to get tough, do the right thing in the face of opposition from some of the residents, for the good of the whole. The water purification system will only provide enough water for those we have, maybe a few more. Food will be at a premium, which means we will have to become self-sufficient." He peered down at Hank's rifle. "I've seen you with that thing, so I'd like you to lead the hunting party, if that's okay with you."

"Hey, sure," Hank replied. "Whatever you need."

"I'll need the elder's backing, which I think I can get. Then, I'll need to get everyone on my side, get them to agree to allow me to lead them."

"Seems to me like you're already halfway there on that score."

Matt nodded. "I'll need to be all the way there. If Emporium is going to survive, make it through one of the worst moments in its long history, then we'll need to make sacrifices. We'll give up some basic freedoms and commit every single hour of every day to this community."

Hank nodded his head. "And the bodies we left in the hills? Your partner and her daughter? The dozens of others? My Rosie, lying out there in the square?"

"We'll bury them here," Matt said, recalling the promise he had made. "In the churchyard. We'll create a special resting place for them. We will never forget those who have fallen."

He thought about Lyndsey, her blond hair caressing her shoulders, her piercing green eyes, and the smile that seemed to cut him in half. He thought of her daughter A.J., with a sass that could bring you to your knees. They had saved him from himself without even realizing it, and it had cost them their lives. He would never let them slip from his memory, forget who they were, and what they meant to him. If he could turn back the hands of time and convince them not to get on that plane, he would do it without hesitation.

There was the sound of gunfire in the distance and a man's agonized screams. Matt grabbed his guns and eyed Hank.

"Ready?" he asked.

Hank stood and hitched his rifle. "I'm ready."

The first shots were fired at 4:30 a.m., and the first man to fall was Hunter Gutierrez, a family man from two streets over who had lived in Emporium for five years. He was walking the perimeter when he spied a group of men approaching. When he turned to call for backup, he was shot in the head by a .308 shell, literally taking the top of his head clean off.

The residents manning the first gun station opened fire, killing two of the approaching group but taking a casualty of their own, a woman in her 50s named Becca Robinson. She was hit in the throat and bled out, right there in the street.

As news of the attack on the west side of Mayflower Avenue spread, more and more residents moved in that direction, leaving the center exposed. The approaching militia had apparently counted on this, and a group of 20 of them descended from the north, taking out one of the guard posts with minimal casualties. They captured old Joe Cooper's house, killing Joe and taking his wife, Betty, hostage.

The eastern perimeter then came under attack, with a group of residents getting pinned down in their guard post, with rifle fire hitting the ground from all directions. Codey had planned well. While the moonlight was bright overhead, the trees on the eastern flank meant that, for the most part, his men were bathed in shadows, and without thermal weapon sights, Matt's snipers —who he'd positioned in the uppermost bedrooms of the surrounding properties—couldn't get a fix on the enemy.

Matt watched from his command post as his people came under attack, seemingly outgunned at least two to one. He hadn't counted on Codey's men being so organized. His strategy surprised him. If he had been a betting man, he would have put down a hundred dollars on the attack coming from the south, hitting them at the point where their forces were less concentrated. Perhaps Codey was smarter than he thought, or he was being advised by people with military experience. Either way, the way it was playing out was troubling to him.

He watched as Roberto took a bullet to the shoulder, slumping behind one of the temporary structures, and listened as an unseen woman screamed out in agony, apparently a victim of a gunshot wound. Sure, they were inflicting damage of their own, but the battle was swinging heavily against them.

"Tucker!" Matt yelled, calling the younger man over to him. The boy stood before him, his rifle across his chest, the pink pimples of pubescent acne on his cheekbones.

"What do you need?" Tucker asked, trying to look as calm as possible.

"It's time."

"What? *Now?!*"

Matt nodded. "That's right. You have to go now."

With that, the young man scampered off, leaving Matt to load his weapons. He couldn't stand by any longer and watch as his game plan was ripped to shreds, and he wasn't in the mood to lose a war to a wannabe gangster and a group of criminals and wastes of flesh.

He headed to the eastern perimeter, moving among the trees, using the shadows as his ally. Ahead of him, two enemy soldiers sat hunched behind a mound of earth, taking potshots at the nearest guardpost. Matt retracted a flare from his belt, ignited it and tossed it in their direction, disappearing among the trees as the red flame illuminated the surrounding area. Immediately, the first guy was hit in the cheek from a sniper bullet and, as the second guy tried to kick the flare away, he was hit—first in the abdomen, followed by a second shot that struck him high in the chest.

Matt moved forward, a pistol in both hands, firing at anybody he encountered. A tall man with snake-like eyes was the first to succumb, taking a bullet in his throat for his troubles, and then Matt moved behind three men who were positioned further along, keeping to the shadows. He shot the first two, and then slit the throat of the third.

However, reinforcements were arriving, and with his position exposed, Matt came under heavy fire. Reluctantly, he retreated, slipping behind the nearest guard post as the ground around him was peppered with gunfire.

"How you feeling?" he asked Roberto, who's arm hung limply by his side.

"I'm okay," he said through gritted teeth. "It's just a scratch."

"I'm going to head to the north," Matt said, "see how they're holding up. Are you and the others okay to hold this area down?"

Roberto nodded, reloading his gun with his good hand. "No problem."

Matt moved across the lawn, ducking among the buildings, his guns drawn. The sun was starting to peek out from behind the horizon, giving everything an eerie glow. The ground was covered in a fine mist, inhibiting visibility for those on the ground; but for Matt's snipers, it worked perfectly. They could see through the thin veil of fog, but their targets couldn't see them. Matt could hear the shots being fired, and the yells as the bullets found their marks, but he knew it wasn't enough. If they were going to survive the onslaught, he needed the next phase of his plan to be put into action.

Sidney joined him as he passed Hank's house, as did Gunn, who looked like he wanted to be anywhere but there.

"They have Betty in there," Matt said. "We have to get her out."

"How many?" Sidney asked, the gun looking too big in his scrawny hands.

"Three, maybe four. You two go round back, I'll take the front."

Gunn gripped his handgun, his hand trembling. "I ain't ever shot a real, live human before."

"Think of it as shooting a rabbit," Matt said. "Only bigger."

The two men moved from building to building, attempting to remain hidden in the mist, but they came under fire from the captured guard post and had to retreat to the rear of Stan Henderson's garage. With the enemy distracted, laying down fire in that direction, Matt was able to come around unnoticed, giving himself a clear view of the male and female unloading on his men. He appeared from the mist behind them, like an angel of death, a ghostly halo of morning sunlight and condensed air moisture surrounding his stetson.

"Lay down your weapons," he roared above the sound of bullets being discharged. "The game's up."

The woman looked at him first, her lips curled in a disgusting sneer, followed by the man, who looked like he'd seen a ghost. As he went to toss his gun to the ground, the woman raised her weapon, but before she could fire, Matt put a bullet in her head and hit the guy in the chest, throwing him backward.

Matt holstered his guns and waved Gunn and Sidney on, glaring down at the bloodied corpses. "Didn't need to go down that way," he said as he turned to the house.

As he approached the building, there were shots from the rear of the property. Matt moved swiftly, kicking the front door in and racing into the living room where a man had Betty on the floor, her mouth bloodied and two of her teeth missing. He put a bullet in the guy's abdomen before he had a chance to discharge his weapon.

"Stay there," he said to Betty, who slumped against the sofa.

He headed toward the kitchen at the rear of the house, where there was the sound of yelling and gunfire. He pushed through the door and watched in horror as Gunn took a bullet to the neck, spilling backward through the screen door. Matt shot his attacker in the back, unloading two more bullets into his torso.

The third man came out from behind the refrigerator, opening fire and missing Matt's ear by a whisker. Matt didn't hesitate, reaching for a kitchen knife and plunging it into his attacker's chest, driving the blade in, all the way to the hilt. The man fell backward through the table, coming to rest by the dishwasher, his eyes vacant and unseeing.

Matt raced out the rear door and went to Gunn, who was lying in the flowerbed, blood pumping from his throat.

"You're gonna make it," he said, but he could see his words were meaningless. Blood was bubbling at Gunn's lips as he tried to speak.

"Did...I....get him?" he asked, grabbing Matt's arm, his grip cold and his fingers without strength.

"Yeah," Matt said. "You got him alright. You saved her, Gunn. You saved Betty's life."

"I...thought...so. I got...him...pretty...good, didn't I?"

"You sure did. Put a bullet right between his eyes."

Gunn's body jerked as blood soaked the ground beneath him, and his eyes glazed over, the hint of a smile on his blood-soaked lips. Sidney sat by the outhouse, a bullet in his hip.

"You're wounded," Matt said, kneeling beside him.

"It'll heal," Sidney replied. "Not sure I'm gonna be much use in a scrap though."

"It's okay. You stay here."

He helped Sidney into the house and sat him next to Betty, who had risen to her feet and was attempting to wipe the blood from her dress.

"They killed Joe," she said, her stare watery and vacant, as if she was still coming to terms with the realities of her situation.

"I'm sorry, Betty."

"You killed them, Mr. Groover? The men who did this?"

"They won't be bothering you again, ma'am." Matt said, tipping his hat. "I just need you to keep an eye on Sidney, if that's okay."

The gunfire outside had intensified, as had the yelling and cussing. The noise was reminiscent of the hateful snarls and rapid gunfire of the streets of Baghdad, without the explosions and the scent of spices wafting among the alleyways.

Matt walked out onto the lawn and stared at the neighborhood. There were fires blazing in some of the houses, bullets peppering the walls, bodies lying in the street, seemingly normal people uttering blood-curdling, hateful screams at men they once considered to be their neighbors.

Matt drew his weapons and paced across the grass, just as the horses emerged from the trees, dozens of them; Hank riding Phoenix, with Savannah on Blackhawk just behind him, Tucker riding a brown thoroughbred, and a group of volunteers Matt had pulled together the previous afternoon who had been riding close by. Hank held the assault rifle they had requisitioned from one of the homes, and he charged headlong into the fray, firing a volley of shells into the approaching enemy. Three men fell instantly, and the others scattered like ants.

Savannah raised her own weapon and shot two men before turning her attention to a group of fleeing women. For his part, Tucker took out an oncoming attacker, shooting him in the stomach. Buoyed by the arrival of the cavalry, the other townsfolk charged, chasing the militia down the street, some of them tumbling onto the ground where they were hauled to their feet by their pursuers and placed in restraints.

Matt gripped his own weapon and strode toward the road. The enemy was outflanked and beating a hasty retreat, but that still left one man who needed to be taken care of—the one person who had organized the town's criminal factions into a vicious, violent army. With the whole town focused on the battle on Mayflower Avenue, he sensed that Codey would make one final play, and that meant *she* was in mortal danger. He slammed home a magazine and headed for the mansion.

CHAPTER TWENTY-SEVEN

Sunlight

The sun was rising above the trees behind the house when he stepped onto the pathway that led across the front lawn. The windows were dark, reflecting the eerie white glow of the morning mist. She stood on the porch, dressed in a white flowing smock, Codey standing at her rear, no doubt holding the muzzle of his weapon to the old lady's spine.

"You make a move, Groover, and she dies," he said.

"The battle's over, Codey. Your plan failed."

"I'll make another one. This doesn't end today."

"I'm afraid it does. This town is mine now."

Codey laughed, long and spiteful. "I knew you had an ego, Groover, but it seems it's far larger than I suspected."

"She said your family were bad news," Matt replied. "I just didn't know how bad."

"You talking about Lyndsey? Shit, she didn't know a good thing when she had it. Mason looked after her, bought her the house, looked after the kid, fed them, gave them everything they wanted."

"He couldn't control his urges," Matt countered. "And that got him killed."

"She abandoned him."

"He abandoned himself."

Codey pushed the elder forward, driving her down the stairs. She tumbled to her knees, crying out as her hands slammed into the turf.

"Steady now," Matt said. "Isla, are you okay?"

The woman peered up at him, forcing a smile. "I've taken harder knocks."

"She didn't love you, you know?" Codey said.

Matt shook his head. "Didn't expect her too. Just wanted to give her and Anna Jayne a life that they deserved."

"So, you got them killed?"

"That wasn't my doing."

"But they were on that plane because of you, right?"

Matt exhaled slowly, recalling Lyndsey's insistence that they come to Pennsylvania so he could see her family shrink. *Did she even want to see her mother? Was that just a ploy to get him to fix his issues, the PTSD brought on by so many years of abuse, lies, and senseless violence in a place thousands of miles from his home? Even though he hadn't caused the plane to malfunction, was he the real reason Lyndsey and her daughter were lying in a shallow grave, up there, alone in the mountains?*

"Shut your mouth, Codey," he said, "before I put a bullet in it."

The gang leader stood behind the stricken elder, and held the gun to her head. "Maybe, but not before I rub this bitch out. Now, I suggest you lower your weapons, Groover, or this whole thing will end with a dead woman on the lawn."

Matt eyed his guns, saw the terrified but resolute expression on the elder's features and the muzzle pressed into her temple. He had no choice but to toss his weapons. He reluctantly dropped them onto the grass and held up his hands.

"You can let her go now," he said. "This is between you and me. She has nothing to do with this."

"What do you think will happen when you take over the town, cowboy?" Codey asked. "You think you'll become president of Emporium or something? Maybe a governor? Is that what you want?"

"This isn't about me," Matt replied. "I just want these people to be safe."

"Until when? Until the army shows up and pushes you out of the chair?"

"Hopefully, yeah."

Codey let out a long, screeching laugh. "Yeah, right. Like you don't have aspirations to rule over these people like some medieval king. I saw you up there in the mountains, telling those poor fools what to do. I watched you surround yourself with willing servants, people too dumb to know what you were up to."

"At least I never killed anyone," Matt snarled. "You killed Hank's wife, slit Otto's throat."

"Yeah, well they had it coming," Codey replied. "Your people needed to be shown the way."

"What way? The way that involves stealing, brutalizing, and ruling people with fear?"

Codey shook his head. "With nobody to enforce the rules, Groover, only the strongest will survive. You can't be soft. Without enough food and water, those people will die in a matter of weeks. Are you willing to lead them to their graves?"

"It won't come to that."

"We'll see."

Matt pointed to the elder. She was on her knees with Codey's gun at her head.

"I dropped my weapons," he said. "Now, you need to let her go."

"I don't need to do nothin'. You're unarmed and we're all alone up here."

Matt stood there, realizing he'd allowed Codey to dictate proceedings, leaving him with a problem to solve. He eyed his guns, which lay on the floor at his feet, and at the elder, who was bracing herself for a bullet.

"It doesn't have to end this way," he said.

"If you're gonna make your move, cowboy, why don't you go ahead and make it already."

Without hesitation, Matt dropped to his knees, grabbing his guns as a bullet whistled past his ear. He rolled onto his side and looked up, just as Levi Cox came running at him from the trees, his weapon drawn. Matt raised his own gun and fired, hitting the taller man in the jaw. He fell to the ground, his eyes wide open in shock, before Matt put another bullet in his temple.

He whirled round and saw Codey coming at him, guns blazing. Matt ducked behind a disused wagon, much of it lying in pieces in the dirt. He dived behind it, just as a bullet struck the rear wheel, and another sent dust flying at his feet. He returned fire, missing by an inch as Codey reloaded, sending another volley of shots into the wagon's side. Matt returned fire once more, striking a swingset in the yard, and grazing Codey's cheek as he dived for cover.

He moved toward the rear of the yard, seeking cover behind a barn that had seen better days. Bullets smashed into the timber structure as the mist danced around his feet. He reloaded one of his guns and let off a succession of shots into the trees. There was a muzzle flash and a bullet struck his right bicep, causing him to drop one of his guns. With his right arm incapacitated, he switched to his left, firing as Codey danced between the pine trees and came up on his left hand side.

Matt moved to the rear of the building and checked his gun. He only had a few bullets remaining, and with his right arm out of action, his aim was compromised. He crouched at the building's edge, waiting for Codey to come at him, but the mist swirled between the trees, the early sunlight glimmering in the distance.

A shadow moved from between them, and Matt let off two shots before standing, walking forward, and firing repeatedly, hellbent on finishing the battle with a flurry of bullets. When the noise died down, and the gun clicked against an empty magazine, there was a sound from behind him, and he turned as the butt of a handgun smashed into his face. He dropped to the ground as a boot connected with his jaw and a fist sent him sprawling.

He peered up at the blurred shadow, the sun at his back, and heard Codey's laugh as he raised his weapon. "This is for Mason," he said as he pushed the muzzle into Matt's face. "And for Lyndsey."

Matt's hand found a piece of two by four with nails protruding from one end and swung it with all his strength, smashing it into Codey's forehead. There was a *thunk* as the gun fell to the floor and Codey's eyes rolled back, blood rolling down his nose as he dropped to his knees. Matt saw the two nails that had punctured Codey's skull, just above his eyebrows, the timber beam hanging from his face. He fell face down in the dirt, his body limp.

Matt rose to his feet and went to the elder, who was standing silently in the distance, her lips bloodied but her spirit evidently intact. "Is it over?" she asked, eyeing the stream of blood running from his wounded arm.

"I don't think so," Matt replied, watching as the sun rose over the trees in the distance, throwing its warm glow over the town of Emporium. He thought of Lyndsey and A.J, of Tiffany and his unborn son, and of his father, murdered in jail after killing a woman who Matt had loved unconditionally. "I'm pretty sure this is just the beginning."

Epilogue

Matt stood and watched as the newcomer and the boy picked among what remained of the buildings that sat outside the perimeter walls of the town. It had been over a year since what they eventually learned had been an EMP strike, and Matt had led his people in creating a fortress in the heart of town, allied with his vision of four guard posts looking out over the valley with a tall fence surrounding their homes. It had been a long 12 months, but they'd come a long way. Heck, he'd come a long way too.

They'd buried the bodies in the cemetery, including those who had fallen in the battle for the town, and he visited Lyndsey and A.J. every day, letting them know how he was doing and how much he missed them.

A few out of towners had arrived since that fateful day. Some they had sent on their way, sensing they were more trouble than they were worth, and some they had allowed in on the condition that they agreed to defend Emporium in the event of an attack. Most accepted. People wanted a home, after all. They wanted what they once had; and while Matt couldn't offer them that, he could offer them food, water, and shelter. In this post EMP world, that was about as good as it got.

"I don't like the look of them," Laura said. She had arrived a couple of month's prior, alone and on the brink of starvation. Her family had been killed by a gang of cannibals, her sister raped and slaughtered. She was an angry person, but someone who Matt felt he could trust with his life. Those types of people were few and far between.

"I don't know," he replied. "There's something about him. Looks like he's ex-military."

"How can you tell?"

"It's just a look," he said. "The way they stand, the way they eye their surroundings, as if anything and everything could be a threat."

"Maybe *he's* the threat," Laura said, mounting her horse.

"Maybe, maybe not."

"I'm heading back to town," she said. "Hank's planning a hunting mission and I said I'd go with him."

Matt watched as the man with the dark hair and rugged features spoke to the young boy with the tanned skin. "You go," he said. "I'm gonna see what this guy has to say for himself."

"You sure about that, boss?"

Matt started walking, his hat pulled low over his eyes, his guns swinging from his belt. "Yeah. Something tells me the two of us are going to have a lot to talk about."

Continue to Series

Link to Book 1

Echoes of the Dark Sun: A Kerrigan's Quest

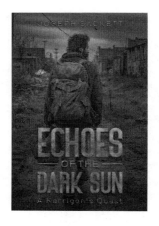

JOSEPH SACKETT

Also By

Dark Skies: A Kerrigan Survival Saga
Book 1: *Echoes of the Dark Sun: A Kerrigan's Quest*
Book 2: *Dark Horizons: A Kerrigan's Journey*
Book 3: *Veiled Shadows: Kerrigan's Redemption*
Book 4: *Fading Light: Kerrigan's Legacy* (Coming Soon!)
Echoes of the Fallen: Matt Groover's Tale *Ties into the second book of the series.
Link to series: https://www.amazon.com/gp/product/B0CF6FH4Y9
Novels
Devils Ridge: Shadows of the Old West

About the Author

Nurtured by the vibrant heart of Minnesota and the streets of Chicago, Joseph Sackett's formative years were steeped in the rich tapestry of America's diverse landscapes. Yet, it was his twenty-year expedition working with the military's special operations that left an indelible imprint on his psyche. It was here that he encountered the harsh realities of human nature, witnessing society's vulnerability and understanding the precarious balance upon which it teeters.

In the face of these stark truths, Joseph found refuge in literature. The stories spun by C.S. Lewis is were the spark that ignited his passion for writing grew over time. His literary appetite led him to the spine-chilling narratives of Max Brooks, a virtuoso of the modern zombie genre, and the grim tale of survival showcased in "The Road" by Cormac McCarthy.

Joseph found profound resonance in these books. He was enthralled by stories of everyday individuals morphing into extraordinary heroes in the face of unimaginable adversity—an echo of the harsh realities he'd observed in his own experiences.

Now, as a writer, Joseph uses his own words as a conduit for this fascination. His writing is a mural depicting mankind's raw vulnerability yet fierce resilience. He infuses his tales with his life lessons, sculpting narratives that expose societal frailties and the indomitable spirit that rises in opposition.

As an author, Joseph extends an invitation into his universe. He invites you to set sail, where every page unravels a fresh insight, each tale bears witness to the resilience of the human spirit. Embrace this journey of discovery. Welcome to the literary realm of Joseph A. Sackett.

Made in the USA
Columbia, SC
16 March 2025

55227085R00200